*From the creators of The Darkest Blog*

# THE CONVENT

## SCOTTSHAK

notionpress
.com

INDIA · SINGAPORE · MALAYSIA

For *Eeya,* my grandma!

# CONTENTS

# Preface

Behold! It's here—the horror book that was once envisioned to reach completion has finally crossed the finish line. Carrying the weight of twenty spine-chilling stories, The Convent is a book designed to take you on a long, winding journey of vivid imagination—one that may just force you to sleep with the lights on.

This collection emerged from one of my websites, The Darkest Blog, which I updated less frequently once I became convinced to turn it into a book. But when life happens, plans stall. An unforeseen medical condition led me into the deepest introspection of my life, and suddenly, publishing anything, let alone a book, stopped making sense.

I was utterly shaken. My ideologies took a backseat. I had once been a fanatic, chasing numerous dreams as if there were no tomorrow. The disease made me stop and breathe, ending a relentless race against myself. I learned that swimming against the flow doesn't always get you anywhere. You have to let the current carry you to reach your destination. The plans set out for us are far greater than the ones we make for ourselves.

The Convent happened on its own accord, taking its intended time. The important thing is that it has finally come to fruition. Some of the stories in this book are true accounts, taken directly from the words of their narrators, with slight variations for the sake of storytelling. Others are figments of my fevered imagination, conjured from dreams or, at times, plucked from thin air for the sheer thrill of terror.

When I began writing this book, I was a sceptic, but the accounts and unexplained events I encountered made me a believer. So much about the supernatural remains beyond our comprehension. Encounters, narrations, and odd experiences all serve to expand our perspectives.

I must begin by thanking my grandmother, Sarda Devi—affectionately known as Eeya—for her riveting storytelling style, which fueled my fascination with the unknown. She was the reason I began hemming vivid imaginations into stories. *Pandubba* is a tribute to her.

I am grateful to the narrators whose real-life accounts allowed me to craft extraordinary stories. This remarkable roster includes Abhishek Ranjan Singh, whose hair-raising accounts helped me write *The Haunting of Saraidih* and *The Shabby Shack*. Yash Gupta's inspiring story breathed life into *Cigarettes and Matchsticks*. I thank my confidant, Harshita Joshi, for enriching *The Convent* and *The Silhouette*. My friend, Abhitosh Kumar, sparked discussions that led to the creation of *The Folklore of Chhayapur*. I also thank my sister-in-law, Timsi Rana, for dictating the events that led to the development of *Under the Banyan Tree*.

The invaluable support of those who directly or

indirectly helped shape The Convent cannot be emphasised enough. My friend Harishyam Gupta's subtle remark led to the creation of *Eight*. A shared adventure at a camp with him and Abhitosh Kumar laid the foundation for the tale. My IT companions in Gurugram—Rahul Ranjan, Punit Gupta, Amit Gaur, Sanyam Tuteja, Abhishek Kumar Jha, and Akshay Saini—engaged in relentless discussions that birthed *Thirteenth Floor*.

I express my profound gratitude to every pillar of support in my life. My mother, Punam Singh, has been my steadfast rock. She is my most attentive auditor who shares my enthusiasm for horror stories. Unbeknownst to her, tales from her childhood have found their way into my writing. I am equally grateful for her prayers and unwavering resolve to rescue her child from the depths of despair. My father, Pramod Kumar Singh, has consistently influenced my decisions to pursue my passion. My brother, Diwya Singh, has provided countless insights into my work and motivated me to keep writing. My sister-in-law, Gauri Diwya Singh, has always championed my work with her incredible support. My niece, Eva—my keenest supporter—has listened to my stories with rapt attention.

I cannot express enough gratitude to my ingenious high school teacher, Mrs. Kirty Kochar, who ignited my enduring love for literature. Her guidance and blessings propelled me to become a better writer and explore the world of poetry, culminating in my first book, Songs of a Ruin.

I am immensely grateful to my publisher, Notion Press, for allowing me to share my voice. This marks my second collaboration with them, and once again, they have proven to be a brilliant platform for writers to showcase their talents. Their invaluable assistance in transforming mere words into tangible work is deeply appreciated.

To everyone associated with this book and to those who have directly or indirectly influenced, inspired, or supported me in my journey as a writer, I extend my heartfelt thanks.

To the readers of this book, the bravest of the brave, who have dared to pick it up, I salute your courage. Brace yourselves for the spine-tingling thrills that await!

May the stories ahead enthral you. Happy reading!

# THE CONVENT

The all-girls School of St. Xavier's Convent was nestled in the mountains of Crescenta. Home to more than two thousand girls from all walks of life, St. Xavier's was renowned for providing superior education. However, like any other institution, it wasn't immune to hidden mysteries. One such puzzling misfortune was an accident that claimed an instructor's life, shaking the convent's very foundation.

Sister Margaret, still in her thirties, had died in an accident that no one spoke about. Perhaps they did not know the details. Mostly, they did not care. Embraced by white roses, Sister Margaret's lifeless body rested in a wooden coffin while children who barely understood death paid their respects. Well, at least they tried.

"Hush! Silence, girls!" Sophia signalled Emily to stay quiet.

Emily, always finding her way into trouble, was now amused by the cadaver's expression. It reminded her of how Sister Margaret's nose puckered when she scolded them in class, whether for not completing their homework or for having untidy pigtails. Margaret's mannerisms were often imitated in the dormitories. Then there was Rose, quite the impersonator, who spared no one.

Emily pointed at Sister Margaret's pale face, mumbled something under her breath, and started snickering. Rose joined in the mischief, both trying to suppress their laughter but failing miserably.

Standing beside the coffin, Sophia almost squeaked in frustration. "This is not good. She is dead. We are at a funeral, for crying out loud!"

The giggling duo fell silent, realising the solemnity of the situation. The dead should not be mocked.

When it was Sophia's turn to pay her respects, she looked at the corpse carefully. *"Poor Sister Margaret! What could have possibly gone wrong?"* she wondered.

Images of Sister Margaret teaching them English flashed through Sophia's mind. She had always been a bright child, completing her homework on time, paying attention in class, and interacting with the faculty regularly. She even attempted to answer challenging questions, which Sister Margaret seemed to appreciate.

Sophia studied Sister Margaret's pursed lips and marvelled at how lifelike she appeared. She looked as if she were merely taking a nap, as though she could wake up at any moment, step away from the coffin, and command them to open their books.

Sister Margaret's distinct features were on full display today, and Sophia couldn't help but gawk at the pale, statue-like figure, wondering how many times she had studied her face up close from where she sat on the first bench.

*"Her eyes... what were her eyes like?"* she thought. *"Weren't they a shade of pale blue?"*

In that split second, Sophia imagined them opening as the deceased sister turned to face her. A deafening silence enveloped Sophia, rumbling like the persistent ring of tinnitus. The world around her had suddenly frozen. Sister Margaret gazed directly at her as if awaiting an answer to a question she had posed in class. Sophia could barely react.

"Move!" someone shoved her from behind.

Her reverie was interrupted by Percy, another student impatiently waiting for her turn. Sophia swivelled around to glance at the corpse once more. Sister Margaret hadn't moved an inch. She lay there lifeless, precisely as a corpse should be.

During recess, the girls were out on the field, playing handball. Sophia sat at the edge of the stairs, observing them. Their faces radiated joy, and everyone appeared fully engrossed and content.

Thoughts brewed in Sophia's mind.

*"How easy it is for people to move on! What is a 'parting' to them? A social gathering of what, an hour? Is that all the time they have to spare for the dead? Or maybe they are cheerful because the deceased is a reminder to celebrate the living. It's strange how people bury themselves in mundane tasks, an ever-chugging engine of pointless acts, embracing superficial indifference to shield themselves from thoughts of death. Just like that, a vibrant, feeling life is extinguished, and the world doesn't even bat an eye."*

Emily pounced on Sophia out of nowhere. "What happened, Sophia? You look lost!" she asked, gasping for breath.

"Nothing, I'm fine," Sophia replied glumly.

"Come join us!" Emily urged.

"I don't feel like it. You guys carry on. I'll go to the study hall."

Sophia declined the offer, picked up her books, and trudged towards the corridor.

"What a killjoy!" Rose whispered as soon as Sophia left.

"Rose! She's our friend," Emily reminded her, still looking in Sophia's direction.

"Yeah, yeah, I know. Come on, let's go!" Rose pulled a worried-looking Emily back into the game.

When Sophia finally managed to push open the heavy door to the study hall, only three other girls were inside. They looked alarmed at first, but upon realising it was just another student, they returned to their magazine, which they had somehow managed to sneak in.

"*Life moves on,*" Sophia thought as she took a first-row seat.

It was a French poem that she attempted to read when she got distracted by all the snickering behind her. She turned around, exasperated, and stared directly at them. Her glare made a statement, and the girls fell silent. One of them signalled the others to take the party elsewhere. The last one to leave pulled the door behind her rather forcefully, causing it to slam shut. Its echo resounded through the empty hall, followed by an unsettling silence.

Sophia turned her attention back to the poem, failing to realise in the first few seconds that she was alone in the study. She was paraphrasing a stanza when that thought crept into her mind. It settled there, lingering.

*"I'm all by myself."* This realisation was accompanied by an unsettling notion of Sister Margaret being alive.

A memory from the past, one of Sister's classes in the same study hall, suddenly erupted in Sophia's mind. The room lit up as the hall was reimagined with students. They were repeating after Margaret as she enunciated an unpronounceable word. She was nodding her head as she walked on.

Just as she was about to pass Sophia, their eyes met, and she stopped. Margaret looked at her expectantly, waiting for her to pronounce the word. The class fell silent. The light dimmed. Sophia struggled to open her lips, unable to answer, wondering if it was too late. Her chin twitched as the syllable tried to escape. It perched on her lower lip and settled there, quivering, waiting for some inconceivable strength to come to its aid. Despite all efforts, it refused to come out.

As anxiety crept in, a whisper brought her back to the empty study hall.

"Sophia!"

She snapped out of her vision and turned around immediately. The large hall, with its dimly lit corners, resembled an auditorium, each row of seats rising higher than the one before. Light bulbs were installed at every intersection, but only one was lit as Sophia scanned the room from one corner to the other. The voice seemed to have come from far away, as if carried from the past.

Considering it a fanciful trick of her mind, she once again buried her head in the book. A surreal thought danced in her mind.

*"What if Sister Margaret's soul never left? What if she loved the Convent so much that she decided to stay?"*

That thought wriggled through her like a slow-moving snake. It slithered from the back of her neck to her jaw, pulling her attention towards the shut door. The only illuminated bulb in the room flickered. Just then, the same whisper she had heard seconds ago came from behind her desk.

That did it for her. Sophia sprang for the door, terrified as if she had seen a ghost. When she pulled the door, it failed to open, so she began frantically rapping at it.

"Open the door! Someone, please! It wouldn't open. Is anybody there?"

She turned around and gawked at the blank space ahead. The bulb flickered again—a dying light. Sophia scanned the room anxiously, her dilated eyes darting from one bench to another. Finally, her eyes settled on the seat she had been sitting on. Her open book was still there. A page lifted on its own before settling neatly back in place. Then the bulb went out.

A scream tore through the corridors of the convent. Several girls came running towards the rattling door.

"Open the door! Please, open the door! Aaargh!" was all they could make out.

The girls pushed against the door as hard as they could from the other side, but it wouldn't budge.

"It won't open! Try from your end," one of the helpers shouted to Sophia.

"Are you alright? What happened?" another asked.

Two teachers arrived upon hearing the shrieks. Realising their efforts were futile, they sent for the peon. By then, Emily had already reached the scene. Known for her strength, she had often showcased her prowess during convent rugby matches.

"Move aside," she ordered. Bracing herself, she threw her weight into one shoulder and rammed the door with all her might. It sprang open.

A petrified Sophia sat on the floor, tears rolling down her cheeks. She looked lifeless as if she had succumbed to dread.

Emily sat beside Sophia and touched her head.

"Sophia?"

Sophia shuddered and looked at Emily. The light was back on. The room was no longer dark. She threw her arms around Emily and broke into sobs.

"Everything is going to be alright, Sophia. I'm here," Emily whispered as she led her away to the dormitory.

Nights at the convent rarely brought promises of sound sleep at the convent—primarily because the girls loved to whisper about ghosts. The very thrill of the topic kept them entertained. But that night was different. The incident with Sophia was on everyone's lips and minds. They imagined the horror she had faced alone inside. Theories and stories were already making the rounds.

Sister Margaret's ghost had already become a tale that was to live on everyone's mind for years to come. It would take a generation of sceptics to get over it, or perhaps just time. Time heals everything, so they say.

Emily and Rose stayed up late with Sophia to make her feel at home. They did everything they could to get Margaret out of her mind. Soon, Sophia had nearly forgotten about the whole affair. Her whimpers softened into laughter as they reminisced about their classroom mishaps, the pranks they played on their teachers and the times they tricked each other.

When the laughter died down and it was time to say good night, Emily said to Sophia, "I'll be right over there. If you need anything…"

Sophia smiled and nodded, then began making her bed.

Two hours later, everyone was fast asleep. More than fifty beds hissed and wheezed, cradling students in preparation for another day's routine. The girls no longer needed alarms because of how accustomed they had become to their regular drills, that discipline ran naturally through their veins. Some might argue that this is how you turn people into robots, wiring them through enforced habits, but ask them how that strict regimen has shaped their lives, and you'll realise it was all worth it.

Sophia found herself in the adjoining cemetery that connected the library to the study hall. The dark had an appetite as it gradually swallowed all the bulbs in the vicinity. She started running towards the convent, but the faster she ran, the farther it drifted away. Suddenly, a hand clasped her leg, sending her tumbling to the ground. She had fallen beside a grave. Trembling, she looked up to read the engraving. It read 'Margaret'.

Sophia jolted awake in the middle of the night, relieved it had only been a dream. She casually opened her eyes and found that she was facing the wall. Just as she was about to drift back to sleep, a familiar whisper echoed in the darkness—the same one she had heard in the study hall.

"Sophia!"

Sophia was wide awake now, her senses razor-sharp. A cold dread settled over her as she became aware of heavy breathing coming from just behind her. Sheer horror gripped her as she deduced it to be none other than Sister Margaret. Paralyzed with fear, she lay still, willing the moment to pass. She dared not turn around, terrified of what she might find.

Minutes stretched into what felt like hours, yet the breathing persisted—slow, deliberate and unrelenting. Whoever it was simply stood there, watching…waiting. Sophia's fear twisted into exhaustion. Her voice, barely more than a whisper, trembled as she managed to plead, "Please…stop."

Tears slipped down her cheeks.

As she spoke, it appeared that the breathing gradually drew away. She could make out the faint rustle of a heavy robe shifting—a slow, despondent walk. The sound seemed to move farther away, towards the dormitory entrance. It lingered there for a moment before finally vanishing down the hall.

Sophia turned to look. Nothing. Just a room full of heavy sleepers. She pulled her blanket close and lay down again, only this time facing the door. As sleep crept over her, a strange heaviness settled in her chest—a quiet, inexplicable sorrow as if she felt sorry for something she couldn't quite understand.

# THE SQUEAKY DOOR

During my final year of college, I moved into a strange rental flat in Bhopal, Madhya Pradesh. The nearby apartments were part of government buildings, arranged in sets of two or four. These were individual units, isolated from one another and surrounded by vegetation. Some units were vacant, while others were occupied; however, the residents mostly kept to themselves.

The grounds belonged to a large corporation that spanned the city. Its employees often rented out their houses to students for extra income. Bhopal was filled with aspirants enrolled in colleges and coaching institutes, all constantly searching for a place to stay.

I longed for solitude, and the rental fulfilled that desire, being situated far from the main road. Moreover, I was fortunate to secure the flat at a very affordable rate. It was a standalone unit, surrounded by shrubbery around the porch, with a garden stretching out in the front. However, its external beauty was deceiving. Inside, the house was damp, its ceiling and walls seemingly crying for help. The paint was peeling, and fungi infested the edges of the bathroom door. Nearly every fourth tile bore cracks as if wearing them like battle scars. In short, everything was in dire need of refurbishment.

The owner had promised to address these issues before handing over the keys. Since I was financially dependent on my parents, I had a fixed monthly allowance to cover my expenses. Given the price I secured for the rental, it felt like a bargain. Aesthetics had never been my primary concern, so I chose to overlook these shortcomings and moved into the ramshackle property.

Weekdays were consumed by the college. I would wake up early and rush out, only to return in the evening. At night, I often took a stroll and called my parents before retiring to bed. Weekends, however, were different—I spent them mostly alone, with little to do around the house.

The human mind is a curious thing—a mysterious concoction of thoughts and perceptions. Plant within it a seed of doubt or a whisper of fear, and it begins to weave a reality around itself—one that might seem absurd to an outsider but, to you, feels so tangible you could almost taste it.

Everything seemed fine during my initial days at the flat, but soon, sleepless nights became a routine. I would wake up in the middle of the night, attuned to the house's sounds. Leaves rustled as if an animal were prancing on the branches of the tree outside. The front porch echoed with the faint crunch of gravel, as though someone were wandering about, plucking flowers. However, the most infuriating noise came from the bathroom door, which squeaked almost every night. The latch was broken, and the wind from the small window would push and pull it like a harmonium. I tried blocking the door multiple times, but somehow, it always broke free, only to start squeaking again.

I started wearing headphones at night, playing songs at a decent volume to drown out the noise. Yet, that squeak had ingrained itself in my mind, always there, waiting for the next note. Sleeping with music on became increasingly difficult, as my brain remained fixated on that tiny disturbance. That unsettling noise had become a part of me, and I, a part of it.

It went on for quite a while. College kept me busy, and I was usually too tired to care. But gradually, my mind began to register stranger things. Upon returning home, I would often find objects out of place. A comb on the floor, a notebook on the bed—though I distinctly remembered leaving it on the shelf.

At first, it all seemed inconsequential. I was too reckless to pay much attention. But a growing curiosity sparked within me, lingering in the back of my mind every night as I lay in bed.

One day, I woke up early and decided to get to the bottom of what was happening behind my back. With a knot of nerves in my stomach, I set up my laptop to face the room—it felt like my very own detective show. I opened a video recording software, set it to capture everything, and left for college.

When I returned in the evening, I was surprised to see the sheets in disarray and clothes scattered around. Then, I noticed the open window.

"Ah! The wind!" I exclaimed.

Eager to check what I had captured, I jumped onto the bed and picked up my laptop, only to find it switched off. I had forgotten to put it on charge.

*"How stupid of me!"* I thought.

After fumbling for the charger, I plugged it in and powered up my laptop. I searched for the video and pressed play.

On the screen, I watched myself primping, humming a popular song before leaving for college. I heard the door click shut as I locked it behind me. Then, an unusual stillness settled in—a silence so absolute it felt unnatural, as if the house itself was holding its breath.

I watched for two to three minutes straight, waiting for something to happen. My heart pounded at an unusual pace. Growing impatient, I fast-forwarded the video since nothing seemed out of the ordinary. Just then, a sound made me immediately pause and rewind.

Playing it again, I heard the same familiar squeak of the bathroom door—the very noise that had disturbed me every night.

It was followed by a thud. I recoiled as a real, identical sound echoed through the house at that very moment. The creaking noise from the video was answered almost instantly by another, this time, a louder, more forceful sound, shaking the entire house before silence reclaimed the space.

Determined to investigate, I put my laptop down, got off my bed, and slowly approached the restless bathroom door. In my haste, I had forgotten to pause the video. The recorded creaks and squeaks continued to play from my laptop as I shuffled towards the bathroom.

When I reached it, I was astonished to find the bathroom door wide open. No wind, nothing this time.

"What the hell? How did the..." I had barely finished my sentence while frantically retracing my steps to the bed when I stopped midway.

An old woman was standing right next to my laptop. Her back was facing me. She seemed to be sniffing as if trying to trace the source of the noise.

Time stopped. I froze with fear.

I stared at that strange old woman for a few seconds as the sound of the creaking door continued emanating from the laptop. She eyed the machine cautiously, curiously. Then, as if sensing my presence, she stopped—

And turned around.

A tattered sari. A charred face. An eye that drooped unnaturally low. That was all I managed to take in before I barged out the main door. I tumbled onto the garden, rolling over before instinctively glancing back, checking if I was being followed. Then, without another thought, I ran. I didn't stop until I reached a friend's house. Five minutes later, I was recounting the entire ordeal in breathless gasps.

I was still shivering when four more colleagues joined in, their eyes gleaming with anticipation.

They begged me to tell the story again. The thrill was too much to handle. Somehow, they convinced me to return to gather my things. I agreed, but only on one condition. They would go in first.

When we reached the house, I refused to go inside. One of my friends stayed with me while the others searched for any signs of an intruder. Finding nothing unusual, they locked the place and brought my essentials out to me. That night, I stayed at a friend's house but couldn't sleep—the creaking, squeaking noise echoed in my head like a relentless bell.

The next morning, I decided to vacate the house immediately. I called the owner and told him what had happened. At first, he laughed, but eventually, he agreed. What unsettled me was how unsurprised he seemed, as if I weren't the first tenant to complain.

Later that day, two of my colleagues helped me pack up. When everything was loaded, I turned for one final look at the house, wondering what mystery lurked behind its guarded walls.

*"What could have happened here? Who was that old woman? Why is she still here?"* Those questions rang in my head, as persistent as the creaking door.

A hand fell on my shoulder. It was my colleague announcing the arrival of the moving truck. I turned away, my resolve shaking, but my vow unbroken—never to return.

# THE CLEANING MANIAC

"Filthy people!" The boy next door spewed curses at Kabir and Vansh.

"At least clean up after yourselves—Jesus, guys!" Jay didn't hold back. He had endured enough mistreatment by his neighbours. It was payback time.

All three were college students who had managed to find rental units right next to their campus. Kabir and Vansh shared an apartment, while Jay had rented a room across from them in the same building. Though he often visited to escape boredom, it always came at a cost.

That day, Jay had discovered how sloppy his neighbours were and decided to push his luck. Once again, he pointed out the smears on the floor—food stains from pulses, curry, and other dishes imprinted there as if someone had deliberately left behind the evidence.

"I've seen you ignore it as if someone's going to come and clean it for you," Jay continued, hoping he finally had the upper hand.

"If it bugs you so much, why don't you clean it yourself?" Vansh retorted.

"Here!" Kabir tossed a cloth at Jay and ordered, "I want this room spick and span."

"Given the number of things you've borrowed from us over the past two months, I think you owe us a good cleaning—at least," Vansh chuckled.

Seeing Jay at a loss for words, Vansh clapped and commanded, "C'mon! Chop, chop!"

It was too much for Jay. He had been humiliated enough.

"Psychos!" he shouted, getting up to leave.

Kabir tried to lighten the mood. "Cleaning, my dear friend, is for weekends. It's an unspoken understanding—nay, a sacred vow—that we, as roommates, have come to terms with."

Vansh gave Kabir a high-five before flopping onto his mattress.

Jay could only mutter, "You guys disgust me. I'm leaving."

At that, Kabir and Vansh lit up almost instantly.

"Oh! Thank you, Lord. Thank you!" Vansh exclaimed, throwing his hands in the air.

"Please don't come back," Kabir added quickly, slamming the door shut on a furious-looking Jay.

Kabir and Vansh's apartment was extremely untidy. In their defence, they claimed that was how they had received it and were merely maintaining its *authenticity*. They slept in the hall, where they had laid out two mattresses on either side, leaving a passage between them—the same spot where the stains could be found. It also doubled as their dining area.

As squalid and reckless as they were, neither bothered to mop until the weekend. Vansh was worse—he would often go five days without showering.

Just as Kabir was about to lie down, there was a knock at the door.

"Must be Jay. Don't open it! Probably looking for a cigarette," Vansh muttered, pointing at the door and hastily hiding his packet.

"Yeah, seriously. We need to be better at hiding our stash," Kabir agreed as he got up to open the door.

To his surprise, no one was there. He stepped out to check the corridor—empty. Outside, rain drummed steadily, punctuated by the occasional crack of thunder.

Convinced it was just Jay playing some stupid prank, Kabir walked over to peek into his room. But there Jay was, lying on his bed, completely absorbed in his studies—just like the studious kid he had always been.

"What the hell?" Kabir muttered to himself as he returned.

"Who was that?" Vansh asked.

"That's weird… no one," Kabir replied, shutting the door behind him.

"Must be Jay!" Vansh said confidently.

Kabir could only nod as he lay down on his bed. Within minutes, both were snoring.

The room would have been silent if not for the distant rumble of thunder, interwoven with the rhythmic patter of raindrops on a galvanised sheet. Occasionally, a frog croaked, as if attempting to contribute to the symphony.

Although Kabir and Vansh always turned off their lights before bed, the dim glow of a streetlight still crept into the room. The main window, where the beams seeped through, desperately needed a curtain. The newspapers they had stuck over it were now tattered and peeling away.

Around 3 AM, Kabir woke up to a faint slurping sound. At first, he thought he was dreaming—the noise seemed distant, almost unreal. But gradually, it drew closer. Soon, he realised it was coming from the narrow passage between their mattresses. It sounded like something was being licked.

Kabir struggled to open his eyes, lost in the labyrinth of his slumber. He lay on his back, hands resting on his chest, staring at the ceiling fan as it rumbled overhead.

His throat was parched. He considered getting up for some water, but the moment he tried to move, he realised—he couldn't.

Vansh slept to his right. *"Could it be him?"* Kabir wondered.

But before he could dwell on the thought, he felt something shift—heavy, deliberate—before the licking resumed.

Kabir tried again to roll over and see what lay to his right, but he couldn't. A surge of strength coursed through him, yet his body remained utterly powerless. He couldn't even tilt his head. All he could see was the ceiling fan looming above, its rhythmic hum the only immediate disturbance—except for that wet, slurping noise.

He tried lifting his hand, but it seemed riveted to his chest. Helpless, he closed his eyes, willing his nerves to relax.

The licking continued. Sometimes, it stopped altogether when the weight shifted, only to return with the same unsettling intensity.

Fifteen agonizing minutes passed before control seeped back into his limbs. As his eyes fluttered open, a jolt shot through him, like a switch had flipped, dragging him back to reality. He wasted no time.

He turned. Nothing.

To his right, Vansh lay undisturbed, snoring softly, his back turned towards him. The passage between the mattresses was empty. The slurping had stopped.

Confused, Kabir tried to shake it off as a bad dream. "But it felt so real!" he thought as he scanned the room one last time, then, just to be sure, turned to face the passage before drifting back into sleep.

By morning, Vansh was already up, getting ready for college.

"Wake up, sleepyhead!" he blurted, as loud as an irritating alarm. "We're running late!"

Exuding lethargy, Kabir rolled over in bed, yawning and stretching. Meanwhile, Vansh moved at supersonic speed, haphazardly gathering his things with one hand while brushing his teeth with the other. He paused, pointed his toothbrush at the floor, and said, "Hey! Weren't we supposed to clean that over the weekend?"

Kabir followed Vansh's gesture towards the passage between the mattresses.

At the speed of lightning, he sat up. His gaze darted to the spot on his right—it was clean. Immaculately so. The food stains were gone. A rush of dread surged through his mind. He had convinced himself that the night before was just a hallucination.

"Who cleaned it?"

The room had been locked all night. The windows were shut.

Kabir's stomach tightened. "What could have possibly caused that?"

It wouldn't be long before he turned into a cleaning maniac.

# PANDUBBA

"What is a *Pandubba?*"

I still remember the night I posed the question to my grandmother. The context, the backdrop, and the time—all the minutiae crystal clear, as if the event was transpiring right in front of me.

Every summer, like clockwork, we visited our grandmother's place. Nights were long, and without electricity, we usually finished our dining chores by eight. Then, we would all head to the roof, where mattresses were laid out for everyone to sleep on.

For us kids, every night would be a story night. We'd start with clapping games, goofing around and disrupting the peace while the elderly struggled to sleep. The only way to quiet us was with a story. Ergo, it is fathomable why it wasn't just the children who eagerly awaited Grandma's tales.

Grandma was always the last to finish her dinner. You could feel the air brimming with anticipation as she made her way to her mattress. We sat in circles around her, restless with curiosity, wondering what tale would unfold that night. I could usually be found pressed up against my seemingly valiant brother, but Grandma's stories could shake even the bravest souls.

Beneath a moonlit sky, the story began. Grandma's snow-white hair flared in the wind as if a ghost were taking shape. My gaze was locked onto her gibbous eyes, which seemed to eclipse everything around me.

The world around us snored, but we had already slipped into the realm of the supernatural.

"Pandubba lives in water!" Grandma replied.

Pandubba, or the water ghost, is a well-known folktale deeply rooted in the villages of Bihar, India. Ask around, and everyone has heard of it. The lore has thrived through mere hearsay, passed down from generation to generation in a formidable timbre. A concept like that might be the product of fanciful ingenuity, but the thrill of hearing it remains unrivalled.

"An exhausted farmer sat by the banks of the river *Punpun*," she continued.

"Is it the one that passes through our village, Granny?" someone asked.

"Yes, that's the one!" she affirmed with a nod, satisfying our curiosity.

"The farmer was sitting on a rock, weary from his journey. He still had a good twenty miles to cover before reaching home. He took out his tobacco and began rubbing it," Grandma went on.

She brought her characters to life, acting them out with precision. Her hands moved exactly as her protagonists' would, drawing us deeper into the tale.

"Just then, a scuffle rose in the water, and he froze. The farmer peered towards the source of the noise, wondering what it was." She paused for emphasis.

"He had failed to notice a man who had appeared out of nowhere and was now standing beside him."

"Who was he?" someone interrupted.

"Shh…." The others hushed the curious one.

Granny looked at the child and smiled as if she had anticipated the impatience she had hoped for.

"He seemed like a commoner," she resumed. "The farmer was taken aback. But when he noticed that the man resembled someone from the village, he relaxed and continued rubbing the tobacco."

"*Do you have tobacco?*" the strange man asked.

In rural areas, sharing items like cigarettes, beedis, and tobacco is a common way to initiate conversations. It eases any potential awkwardness, as most discussions in the countryside begin with an offer or exchange.

"*Can I have some tobacco, please?*"

"The farmer nodded and kept rubbing the tobacco. The stranger pleaded again, uncertain if the farmer had actually agreed to share."

*"Please, some tobacco."*

It is the way my granny said it that made me anxious—the way she would rub her hands, embodying the Pandubba itself. My imagination failed to go beyond the image she projected.

To a child, Pandubba bore the face of my grandmother. Maybe it looked like her when she had her hair untied, maybe it had her grey eyes. Maybe it cajoled people into giving it tobacco, just as she would. Her gestures had already etched the image of the water ghost into my mind.

"He pleaded fervently until the farmer finally relented and offered him some."

A collective gasp pierced the night. We all knew something terrible had happened.

"That was it! That's something you don't do. You never offer Pandubba anything."

"Why?" my brother asked, his voice barely above a whisper.

"He feeds on your generosity. That's the only way he can get close to you—only when you offer him something, especially when you stretch out a helping hand."

Her sharp gaze lingered on each of us, sending shivers down our spines.

"That was the farmer's final mistake. The Pandubba seized his hand and yanked him into the depths of the river. The farmer couldn't fight back—the grip was too tight. Pandubbas are strongest in the water."

Our mouths hung open as Granny's words settled over us like a thick fog.

"Soon, the farmer began gurgling water, his mouth filling as he was dragged down. He could sense the light in his eyes dimming as he was drawn to the riverbed, away from the shallows."

"Then, what happened?" the children whispered, trembling.

"The Pandubba held the farmer against the riverbed, then filled his eyes, mouth, ears, and nose with sand, covering his face completely, to keep his body from coming floating to the surface."

I was already imagining it happening to me. Frantically, I covered my ears and nose with my tiny hands.

"That's how a Pandubba renders you powerless. You arc unable to move. That's how you die—a slow, mortifying death," she declared, her glare lingering on each of us.

"Never go near the water alone—especially at night. If you see a stranger near the river, stay away," Granny warned before leaving us alone with our thoughts.

Sleeping after her tales was always a challenge. My naive mind would conjure up its own stories after hers—a dreary aftermath that painted itself onto the canvas of my imagination, a picture I would carry for a lifetime. Perhaps, one day, I would pass it down to future generations, preserved in writing, the most powerful way to keep history alive.

Even after so many years, her stories still breathe. Even after her passing, she somehow managed to leave behind a piece of herself. For that, I remain grateful.

# CHECKOUT

"C'mon, dear! There's no such thing as ghosts. Don't you know that by now? I mean, you're a grown-up, for crying out loud, and you still believe in this nonsense?" Mike was trying his best to talk sense into Christy, whose head was still clouded with doubt.

"No, but I'm just saying…" Christy fumbled for a reason.

"Okay, answer this," Mike cut her off. "Have you ever seen a ghost yourself?" He looked directly at Christy, half-expecting an answer.

"No, but Karla said…" Christy tried to bring Karla, their 60-year-old neighbour, into the conversation, but Mike interrupted again.

"Forget about what Karla said," he continued. "She doesn't know what she's talking about. She's been watching far too many horror movies."

Mike hated how Karla kept filling Christy's head with balderdash. Their argument continued as they got out of the car and made their way to the reception desk.

Christy and Mike Smith, both in their mid-thirties, had different occupations—Mike owned a car company in Denver, while Christy was a homemaker.

The Smiths carried their two-year-old son, Zack, in their arms. The baby, his teary eyes observing the commotion, was now on the verge of bursting into tears.

It was the holiday season, and the Smiths were en route to visit Christy's parents' house in Ogden, Utah. Despite Mike's impeccable navigation skills, they got lost after he decided to take a shortcut. Their new plan was to find a hotel for the night and resume their journey in the morning with better visibility.

"You could have stayed on the highway," Christy complained again.

"For the last time—I know the way! I just drive better in the morning."

They had managed to find a hotel, thanks to a faint light flickering in the dark. Mike had taken a sharp turn, following a muddy lane to get there. As they navigated, the ominous surroundings sent chills down Christy's spine. Her reluctance to go any further exasperated Mike. That's when they started bickering over ghost stories.

From the looks of it, it was a shabby old hotel. A frail old man sat at the reception desk, reading a newspaper. He had light grey hair and despondent eyes. His brown waistcoat was torn in several places, and one could tell he badly needed a shower.

The old man looked up from behind his glasses and groaned, "Yes?"

"We're looking for a room for the night," Mike said.

Two minutes later, the Smiths were following the receptionist down a dark hallway. The old man lit a lamp, casting flickering shadows along the corridor.

The couple continued to argue. The little one could only take so much—Zack started crying. His wails seemed to stir something behind the shut doors, prompting restless shuffling, as if his cries had disturbed slumbering souls.

The old man opened a door, revealing a single bed.

"What? We're looking for a room with two beds," Mike clarified.

The old man groaned. "All the rooms here have single beds. You either adjust or take another room."

Christy's eyes flared, "Are you serious?"

The old man ignored her. Mike, still annoyed with Christy, was the first to break the silence. "Fine! I'll take the next available room."

Christy was too furious to argue. Strange places always worried her, but she chose to remain silent, not wanting another fight. She agreed, finding solace in having Zack for company.

Upon entering the room, she frowned, "Why are the lights so dim here?"

The old man groaned in response and silently left her with the child to settle in.

Meanwhile, Mike stood at the door of the room Christy and Zack had entered, waiting. The old man unlocked the adjacent room, and Mike stepped inside to inspect it.

"Could you switch on the lights?" he asked, squinting into the darkness.

The old man fumbled with the switch but to no avail.

"Ah, perfect! So there are no lights here," Mike scoffed.

"I'll change the bulb right away," the old man assured him as he slowly turned towards the corridor.

Watching him move at a sluggish pace, Mike blurted out, "You know what? Forget it. I'm heading straight to bed anyway."

He switched on his phone's flashlight, felt around for the wardrobe, hung up his shirt, located the bed, and threw himself onto it. Exhausted, he was snoring in no time.

Meanwhile, in the other room, Christy was preparing for bed. A loud thumping noise echoed from the wall, and she wondered if Mike was trying to check on her. As Zack crawled restlessly on the bed, searching for the perfect spot, she reached for the door.

Peeking out cautiously, she scanned the dimly lit corridor. A lone struggling bulb flickered in one corner. Turning to look down the opposite end, she nearly shrieked. The old man stood right in front of her.

"You scared me!" Christy barely managed to say.

"Do you need something?" the old man asked, his gaze lingering on her nightgown.

"No, thank you," she replied, instinctively pulling the fabric closer around her.

He leaned in slightly and added, "If you do, just press 9."

"Okay, I will. Thanks," she said quickly, shutting the door. The encounter left her disconcerted. Now, she was too scared to visit Mike, and the dark corridor was reason enough to stay put.

"That guy gives me the creeps," she murmured to Zack, who was busy rubbing his eyes.

As she applied lotion as part of her bedtime routine, it happened again—the loud thump in the stillness of the night, enough to jerk her upright. She glanced at Zack, who was already fast asleep.

Then, another thump.

She was on her feet in an instant. The sound seemed to be coming from the wall—possibly from Mike's room. Was he trying to play a prank at this late hour?

"Honey? Is that you?" she called out, stepping towards the wall and knocking back.

The wall struck back—this time, even louder. Her breath caught in her throat. Heart pounding, she rushed to the bed and clutched Zack tightly.

Christy left the lights on before slipping beneath the sheets. All those horror movies she had watched growing up began replaying in her mind. Karla's stories resurfaced—tales of hauntings in the woods. This strange hotel seemed to be right at the heart of them. If only Mike had listened to her.

The thumping had stopped—or perhaps it had simply been replaced by the pounding of her own heartbeat. She lay still, gripped by the whirlwind of her gasps, holding Zack tighter. Then, in the deafening silence, she heard hushed whispers— muffled voices drifting in from the corridor.

Christy pulled the blanket down to breathe properly. As she did, a sharp gasp escaped her. The door to her room stood wide open, exposing the darkness beyond. Her eyes widened in sheer terror.

"Maybe that creepy old man opened it," she thought, still reeling from the shock.

Heart hammering, she climbed out of bed and crept towards the door. A glance outside revealed that the corridor light was no longer on, leaving the hallway utterly drowned in darkness. Peering into the void unnerved her even more.

Christy locked the door again, ensuring it was fastened properly. She checked the room to confirm everything was in place and peeked under the bed to make sure nothing had crept in while the door was open. Then, she picked up the receiver, only to find the phone was dead. She didn't have a phone of her own, leaving her with no other choice.

She returned to bed, still fuming at Mike for abandoning her and Zack like that. They could have managed in the same room somehow if they hadn't been fighting.

She seethed at being stranded in a strange place that creaked and thumped, where the phones didn't work, and where sleep felt impossible. A sinking feeling welled up inside her as she realised it was barely midnight, with hours still to go before they could leave that forsaken place.

"What am I going to do? Oh, Mike! Where are you?" she choked out, her voice trembling as tears welled in her eyes.

In the other room, Mike had an uneasy nap. He woke abruptly, startled by a sudden nudge on his hand, as if something had brushed against him. Squinting, he glanced around, groping for his phone in the dark, but couldn't find it.

"Maybe it was a dream," he thought before turning over and burrowing into the bed again.

Not long after, there it was again—a cold touch that could rouse even the deepest sleeper. It was so vivid that Mike sprang up and shouted, "Who's there?"

As he spoke, he felt a force push his arm, followed by a nudge from behind, then a shove from the right. Perplexed, he tried to discern if he was still dreaming.

A sharp slap on his bare chest settled it. The sting knocked him back, and now he was wide awake— gawking into the darkness, gasping for breath, reeling from the shock of whatever had just invaded his room.

He scrambled until his hand found his mobile phone. Fumbling, he switched on the flashlight and swept it across the room.

Nothing.

He checked under the bed, then opened the cupboard. Still nothing. Finally, he examined the door latch—it was bolted.

It was the strangest thing he had ever experienced. He moved towards the wardrobe mirror to check for a mark where he had been hurt. A large red imprint was spread across his chest.

That's when Mike heard the thump against his wall. It was too much for him. He dashed for the door, his mobile slipping from his grasp in his frantic attempt to flee. It felt as if something was chasing him.

He flung the door open to complete darkness. Remembering that his wife's room was next to his, he moved along the wall, expecting to find a door—but there was none. Just more walls.

The dim light from the lobby was the only thing he could see.

*"Why am I not moving?"* he struggled to make sense of what was happening.

Despite using all his strength, something seemed to be pulling his other hand, preventing him from leaving.

The walls ahead stretched endlessly. Mike was almost running, convinced he was getting closer to the lobby, but the harder he tried to move forward, the stronger the force pulling him back became. He felt many hands gripping him, stopping him from leaving. With each icy touch, the pain in his body intensified. He was too terrified to look back.

Mike was beginning to despair when he shouted with every ounce of strength he had left, "Christy! Help!"

Just then, a door to his left flung open, as if a portal of light had suddenly burst into existence. The brightness was blinding. His knees buckled, and he collapsed.

"Mike! Mike! Are you alright?" It was Christy.

She rushed out of her room and lifted him from the ground. At first, she was taken aback by the sight of him—his body covered in red marks, fresh wounds that looked as if something had tried to claw at his flesh.

Supporting him, Christy helped Mike to his feet. He finally turned to look at whatever had been chasing him.

Nothing.

The darkness had returned, thick and suffocating. Silence pressed in, erasing all traces of what had just occurred.

Mike was drained, sweat dripping down his face. He looked like he was in pain as he stared into the dark corridor ahead. Summoning what little strength he had left, he acted on instinct.

"Let's get the hell out of here!"

Christy rushed inside to grab Zack and was back within moments.

"What is this place?" She asked as they hurried towards the lobby.

At the reception, the old man slowly lowered the newspaper. His expression shifted from indifference to unease as he took in their dishevelled state.

"What the hell is this place?" Christy shouted, her voice raw with fury.

The old man blinked, his expression unreadable, "What happened? Are you alright?"

"There is something wrong with this place. We want to leave. Now," she demanded.

The old man exhaled slowly. "Alright." He pulled out his register and pointed at their names, "Just sign here to check out. No refunds."

"What? Are you serious?" Christy was about to create a scene when Mike stepped in, preventing further confrontation.

He moved forward, snatched the pen from the old man's hand, and signed where he was instructed. The old man leaned in and whispered, "You should have listened to your wife. Usually, they don't bother people. They keep to themselves. You provoked them."

Mike frowned. "What… What are you saying?"

But the old man simply stared into his eyes.

"Mike, are you done? Let's go!" Christy tugged at his arm impatiently.

They had nearly reached the gate when the old man suddenly shouted at the top of his voice.

"Madam, I believe you're taking something that belongs to my hotel," he said, gesturing towards her shoulders with his eyes.

"What do you mean, I—" Christy's words caught in her throat as she realised the weight in her arms felt all wrong. A cold shiver crawled up her spine as she looked at what she had been carrying.

It wasn't Zack.

She had been holding a pillow the entire time. A bloodcurdling scream tore from her throat as she dropped it.

At that moment, Zack's cries echoed from the corridor they had just fled.

Mike turned to the old man, but instead of concern, the man's face twisted into a grin.

He shrugged. "They gotta feed."

Without a moment to spare, Mike charged back into the inferno of darkness, bracing himself for whatever awaited. The empty hotel reverberated with the sound of Christy's helpless cries.

# THE SHABBY SHACK

Sachar was still in his twenties when he decided to spend his mid-summer break at his uncle's house in New Delhi. A gregarious and headstrong young man, he loved exploring new things. He was also highly assertive when it came to getting things done and was always prepared for whatever life threw his way—all reasons why his uncle found him incredibly useful whenever he visited.

Kailash, Sachar's uncle, was a 42-year-old man who lived with his wife and three children in a rented house on the outskirts of the city. After years of diligent saving, he finally managed to purchase a plot for his family. In no time, he began construction on their new home. Sachar's visit was warmly welcomed, as Kailash needed an extra pair of hands.

Kailash was a manager at a paper firm, which left him little time to oversee the daily construction work. Sachar's presence was a relief, as Kailash could now delegate crucial tasks to him.

Since the new building under construction was quite far from their rental home, Kailash and Sachar often stayed overnight in a dilapidated shack adjacent to the site. From there, they had a clear vantage point to monitor the ongoing work, where labourers toiled daily to complete the job. They took turns sleeping at the shack, with Kailash's wife preparing dinner for whoever stayed over. With the countryside air streaming through the shack's window, opening their tiffin boxes felt like a picnic.

Though neglected and unpainted, the little shack had a single room where mattresses were stowed on the floor. It became their resting place as they overlooked the workers labouring away.

Mani, the contractor overseeing the construction, was a young and amicable man. Sachar enjoyed his company, especially for the stories he told. The two often shared food and talked late into the night. On many occasions, Mani would crash on the second mattress in the room.

During the daylight hours, most of the masonry progressed under the sun, while nights were spent in a familiar rhythm of childhood anecdotes and wheezing snores. As the days passed, the house neared completion. One evening, it was Sachar's turn to stay over. His aunt had prepared a delicious dinner, which he and Mani devoured before settling into conversation. Mani reminisced about his college days, spinning tales until their exhaustion took over, and they fell asleep.

In the middle of the night, Sachar woke from a bad dream. He tried to go back to sleep but couldn't. Mani's snores filled the room. Restless, Sachar let his mind drift to his own college life. He had made some good friends, too. Soon, the summer vacation would be over, and they would reunite for more late-night escapades.

Sachar started recalling his first day at college—how overwhelming it had been at first, and how, gradually, everything had begun to settle. He had felt homesick at the start of his journey, but now, his hostel felt like another home.

Suddenly, he realised he had been lost in thought for too long. He needed to shut off his brain and go back to sleep. But no matter how hard he tried to calm his mind, he couldn't. His restless thoughts aside, Mani's snores were loud enough to wake the dead.

Sachar turned to face Mani, only to find him lying with his back to him, facing the wall. Thinking a light tap might wake him, Sachar reached out and poked his shoulder.

"Mani?" he whispered.

The moment his finger made contact, Mani's head twisted towards him. But his torso remained facing the wall.

Sachar froze.

Mani's eyes were wide open, staring at him with a look of loathing and resentment.

Before he could react, an invisible force erupted from Mani, slamming into him and pinning his hands to the floor. Sachar could barely move. The power radiating from the entity was unlike anything he had ever encountered. Or had he somehow grown weak?

He fought with all his might, struggling against the invisible force, but the harder he pushed, the more helpless he became. He opened his mouth to scream—only to realise he had lost his voice.

He lay on his back, fighting the entity that seemed to be pressing down on him, its presence seeping into his very bones. An unimaginable pain shot through his wrists. With no way out, Sachar—a devout man—cried out the name of his deity.

The moment he did, the crushing force pinning him down vanished.

It was as if a massive weight had been lifted from his body. He gasped for breath, sprang up, and switched on the lights. Nothing.

His eyes darted to Mani, who still lay facing the wall, his head and torso intact. Sachar shook him awake. Mani stirred groggily at first, but upon noticing Sachar's frantic state, he sat up, listening intently.

"Did you feel that too?" Mani asked after hearing Sachar's account. "Something has been bothering me in this room for a while now. I thought I was going crazy."

They remained awake for the rest of the night, sleepless, yet fortified by each other's wakeful presence.

The next day, he recounted everything to his uncle, but Kailash only laughed it off.

Sachar never returned to that place again. He left to stay with his parents, using college term work as an excuse.

In the years that followed, he often told the story to his friends. Every time he did, goosebumps prickled his skin, transporting him back to that shabby shack, reliving the nightmare all over again.

Kailash has long since moved to his new house with his family. Sachar has visited many times and even stayed over. The shack still stands where it always has, visible from their balcony.

Even now, he finds himself staring at it, wondering what secrets it conceals.

He has often brought it up during family suppers more than once. Nobody ever seems to care.

# Matchsticks and Cigarettes

It was an odd place for a college. The town had clashed with the government numerous times during the planning phase, citing the dangers of wild animals and the disruption of the forest ecosystem, but to no avail. Eventually, the Smile Institute of Science and Technology established itself comfortably right in the heart of Chambal's dense forest.

The forest was home to wild animals. It was their hunting ground, untouched and primal. But, as with every corner of the world, mankind had sprawled across this land too, claiming it as if they were the rightful owners of the planet.

Colleges tend to create life around them. Small shops and kiosks selling tea, newspapers, and cigarettes sprang up effortlessly. A one-way road cut through the jungle towards the city, where students thronged for stationery, laundry, food, and other essentials. However, it was a five-kilometre walk to get there.

Despite human encroachment, the creatures of the forest still prowled, fighting for dominion. Man visually demarcates his life and tries to separate himself from nature, but when night falls, all such fabricated frontiers dissolve.

News of countless animal attacks in the area spread quickly. Rumours spread like wildfire about unknown creatures lurking in the woods. But has that ever stopped a teenager from venturing out? The very thrill of walking the knife's edge is where teens find their fervour.

The edge of the forest was always bustling with people. The precinct's regulars were students, which is why many shops remained open even in the wee hours. Business was booming, and Prakash Sharma, the owner of a small dhaba, wasn't complaining.

Sharma's restaurant stood at the forest's edge, where the college road met a crossroads. His dhaba catered to every night owl dissatisfied with their cooks.

A group of seven students—Jeetu, Tushar, Dinesh, Saurav, Karthik, Mukesh, and Dheeraj had turned the eatery into their second home. To satisfy their late-night hunger pangs, they didn't mind walking the five-kilometre stretch.

Five of the kids got stoned that night after Jeetu managed to score a reefer from somewhere. They snuck out through Karthik's balcony—their usual escape route—after slipping the guard a twenty.

Once they were at a safe distance from the college, they ambled down the main road. Saurav started a song, and everyone chimed in. They sang for a while before the conversation drifted to the girls studying at the nearby convent. Soon, they were teasing each other, cracking jokes between bursts of laughter.

The journey felt like something out of a dream. None of them had any real memory of how they made it through the forest. Their singing and dancing made them look like a wandering troupe on its way to a performance. The stage was set at Sharma's.

The joint made them ravenous. The boys devoured everything Sharmaji had on the menu.

"Screw it! I'm having another round of Chicken Tikka—for dessert!" Dinesh declared after finishing his meal.

"You had that yesterday too," Tushar pointed out.

"And it was good!" Dinesh shot back.

When everyone was done eating, they rested for a while. The thought of walking back weighed on them more than their stuffed stomachs. But the journey was inevitable—they couldn't afford to get caught. Getting caught would mean an end to their little night-out adventures.

Reluctantly, the gang hit the road, their conversation meandering between random topics. Someone brought up their college faculty.

"Who's the best?" Dheeraj asked.

"Neelima, Ma'am! Hands down," Mukesh answered without hesitation.

Everyone agreed in unison.

"I love the way she looks at us," Tushar added with a dreamy smirk.

The night came alive with their laughter. The full moon peeked at the students through the branches as they strolled down the deserted path. On both sides of the road thrived different kinds of wild plants, beyond which the forest would expand.

As they walked on, Trinity Church loomed to their left, its silhouette barely visible. A dim light flickered from inside. It was only after passing the church that the pathway narrowed slightly, the trees pressing in closer, their shadows weaving an eerie gloom.

Tushar was the first to steer the conversation towards the supernatural. Soon, they were discussing the darker mysteries of the woods. They rustled through historical leaflets, revisiting rumours that had percolated in the city—how things were always hiding in the bushes, the countless serial murders from months ago, and the unfounded sightings of witches.

Saurav reassured them, "Seven of us—we can handle anything."

With that, Karthik started counting and suddenly shrieked, "Guys, we're only six!"

Befuddled, everyone began counting. His claim was quickly overruled—Karthik had forgotten to count himself. As he made a vain attempt to prove himself right, a fog began to form about fifty meters ahead. No one was paying attention until someone pointed it out.

"Hey! Where did that come from?"

Everyone stopped to look at the white mist ahead. Just then, a matchstick struck in the fog. The tiny flame flickered mid-air. There was nothing around it—just the fire burning bright, swaying as if trapped in a shared hallucination. Then, two cigarettes followed, blocking the flame, their red tips glowing as they were lit.

Something took a long, deliberate drag before the matchstick died out, leaving only the two smouldering cigarette tips, pointed directly at them.

Tushar whispered under his breath, "Can you see it too?"

"Yes... What are we going to do?" Dinesh asked, his voice trembling.

"Keep walking," Saurav muttered.

As they moved forward, one of the cigarettes drifted towards the edge of the road before disappearing. The other remained where it was, still puffing. The boys could easily distinguish the cigarette smoke from the fog. Since they smoked too, it was easily recognisable to them.

Whatever it was, it wasn't afraid of a group of seven college boys walking in its direction.

When they were about twenty meters away, the boys saw the cigarette fall to the ground, its cinders releasing sparks in all directions. Then, there was nothing but mist.

As they drew closer to the spot where all the mysterious action had just occurred, a strong scent of cigarettes lingered in the air. The smell was so strong it felt almost tangible, as if someone had just smoked a pipe.

They had almost passed the spot when one of them noticed a man sitting by the edge of the road. No head was attached to his torso. Smoke emanated from where his head should have been.

Tushar whispered under his breath, "Guys! Can you see it too?"

"Yes… Shh… keep walking," Dinesh whispered back.

"Ignore it. Don't look at it," Saurav advised.

"Guys, there's smoke coming out of his head…" Mukesh remarked.

"Shh… don't!" Dinesh silenced him as they crossed the entity.

Everyone had seen the headless man except Dheeraj. He had no clue what everyone was whispering about, so he blurted out, "Where? Where? I want to see it too!"

As he turned around to look, it was too much for the others. They blasted off like cannonballs. Not a single person stopped until they reached their college gate. They turned around to check if they were being chased before sneaking back into their hostels.

Later that night, all seven of them assembled in a room to discuss the inconceivable event that had defied their reefer effects. Everyone's story checked out—they had all seen the same thing.

They made fun of Dheeraj for how he had almost gotten them into trouble and laughed about how they had run with all their might, hearts pounding as if the headless man was chasing them.

It was almost three when they finally retired to their beds, terror still gripping their hearts. Many of them couldn't sleep.

At a quarter past four, Saurav felt the urge to smoke. He went to the corridor and found Karthik, who was on his way to the water cooler.

"Rough night," Saurav remarked.

"Yeah," Karthik responded.

"Let's light one," Saurav suggested.

They went to Karthik's terrace, which overlooked the main gate and the road beyond. The guard seemed to be asleep on his chair.

Saurav and Karthik shared the cigarette since they only had one. Saurav found a matchbox with just a single matchstick left.

"Make it count," Karthik winked.

Saurav lit it up. With the very first puff, images from the road came rushing back to his mind. The similarities were uncanny.

As the smoke dispersed, Saurav saw Dinesh on the road, staring at him.

"Dinesh!" he almost shouted.

"You good, bro?" Karthik asked, noticing Saurav looking tense.

Saurav glanced back at the road—nothing. In the blink of an eye, Dinesh had vanished into thin air.

Confused, Saurav bolted to Dinesh's room, panic tightening his chest. Dinesh was still in his bed, sleeping like a baby.

"You alright, man?" Saurav asked, shaking him gently.

"Let me sleep," Dinesh muttered, annoyed, before burrowing deeper into his blanket.

"*Am I seeing things?*" Saurav thought to himself.

Still shaken, he rushed back to Karthik's room and scanned the road again.

"Dude, you're freaking me out. You okay?" Karthik asked, clearly worried.

Saurav searched the road over and over, convinced he had seen Dinesh standing there. But no matter how hard he looked, there was no trace of him. Finally, he turned to Karthik, took a deep breath, and forced himself to sound calm.

"Yeah… I'm fine now."

Karthik held out the cigarette. Saurav stared at the glowing embers for a long moment before shaking his head.

"I quit."

# THE ORCHARD WITCH

Near the village of Ahawapur stood a tall statue of an old man, carved to perfection. The statue depicted a Pandit dressed in a *dhoti* and *kurta,* and his head bowed low as though walking towards the village. However, it wasn't a complete statue—the old man's legs were sculpted into the base, an oddity that often raised questions among the village kids.

The statue was situated just outside the village, a fixture one had to pass when entering or exiting. Covered in layers of dust, it bore the marks of antiquity. Over time, it had become grimy from the relentless bombardment of bird droppings. Enveloped by a circular platform, it presented a rather uninviting sight, deterring anyone from lingering. People briskly navigated past the statue, and some even opted for a different trail to avoid it altogether.

For an eight-year-old village boy named Aman, the statue had always remained a mysterious subject. He had passed the work of art countless times but had never discovered anything strange. The fact that no one talked about it only added to his frustration. Questions such as why the statue was built outside the village and why everyone behaved strangely when asked about its history had kept him awake on many sleepless nights.

One late afternoon, on his way back from the shop, Aman noticed a peculiar young man standing by the statue, piquing his curiosity. He quickened his pace, hoping to get some answers from the stranger.

The young man's reverie was broken when he heard approaching footsteps. A streak of disappointment flashed across his face as he looked at Aman—he had been expecting someone else.

Aman was taken aback by the stranger's face. There was something familiar about it, but he couldn't quite place it. The stranger wore grey trousers, a grey overcoat, and a white collar that peeked out, revealing the colour of his shirt. He also had a matching hat, which he held to his chest, and a small bag hung tightly from his arm.

Initially shy, Aman held back his thoughts until he noticed the stranger mumbling something. Overcome with curiosity, Aman stepped forward and broke the silence.

"Do you know this man?"

The young man stopped mumbling, took a deep breath, and replied without looking in Aman's direction, "My father."

"What happened to him?" Aman asked immediately. The young man chose not to reply and closed his eyes once again.

"Where are his legs?" was the follow-up question to the one left unanswered.

"Go away, kid. Leave me alone," the young man muttered, struggling to concentrate.

"What happened to him? How did he die?" Aman questioned relentlessly.

The young man shot a glance at Aman and said, "You don't know, do you?" Aman shook his head in denial.

The young man asked, "Haven't you heard about the orchard witch?"

The reference rang a bell, but Aman did not know the story behind the name. He chose not to respond.

"Are you really from this village?" the young man raised a brow as he sat on the platform beneath the statue.

When neither of them spoke for a while, the young man continued, "What you see around used to be an orchard of banyan trees. The roots were so firmly riveted to the ground that it took months to uproot the entire orchard."

"Why did they uproot it?" the child asked immediately.

The young man scoffed at Aman. "Ah! Curiosity! You know, I used to be a curious child like you. But you have to be careful with it. Don't go to places where you're not supposed to be."

"But why did they cut down all the trees?" Aman reiterated, ignoring the stranger's remark.

The young man looked at Aman and said, "To tell you that, I have to narrate the whole story about the orchard witch."

"Tell me!" the boy persisted.

The young man closed his eyes, dreading to turn back the dial of time, yet his purpose of visit demanded that he do so. He took a deep breath before beginning the story, "Twenty-five years ago…"

To reach Ahawapur, one had to cross a vast orchard of banyans, a feat especially challenging at night. Villagers claimed to have experienced unusual activities while passing through the orchard.

Sceptics dismissed these claims, attributing them to either thugs hiding in the branches to rob people or the commotion of restless birds disturbed by the slightest noise. However, within a few days, they would all be proven wrong.

The Sharma family of the village had a dispute over their land. One of their youngest members, Ekant Sharma, a 33-year-old man, decided to part ways with his family, taking his share of the land. He wished to engage in farming and build his own house. Following a major disagreement, Ekant moved to a rental in the city with his wife. They planned to return once their house was completed.

After finalizing which portion of the land belonged to him, Ekant set out at once to begin construction. He erected a boundary wall to fortify his share and then built a small house at its edge. The patch of land he acquired was right next to the banyan orchard. During the construction phase, Ekant made multiple visits, and things seemed to be progressing as planned.

Like most villagers, Ekant was a sceptic. He ignored every warning about the orchard being haunted, dismissing the stories as mere superstition, and went ahead with his initial plan. Once a boundary wall and a small room were completed, Ekant placed a bed inside to enjoy the tranquillity of the orchard during his visits. He relished spending peaceful days, with a cool breeze flowing through the window that he had specifically requested to be built.

"The Fat Sharma." That's what everyone called him, especially the village kids. Upon hearing that Fat Sharma had been living alone near the banyans, the village kids began messing with him every night. They would make hooting noises or occasionally knock on his door and run away, drawing pleasure from the curses that followed.

That night wasn't supposed to be any different—only this time, I had accompanied the mischievous kids to witness the fun firsthand. When we peeked through the window blinds, we were surprised to see that Ekant Sharma had brought his wife from the city. Hoping to witness some action, the kids lined up, standing on top of each other near the window. Amid the mischief, someone let out a hooting noise, and the entire group bolted, laughing as they ran, leaving me hanging at the top of the window, balancing on my elbows. I hung there, frozen.

Fat Sharma came out, cursing, coughing and spitting in the direction of the village before returning to bed. But what I saw next was beyond anything I had ever imagined. Ekant had started kissing his wife's legs—only, it wasn't his wife anymore. Unbeknownst to Sharma, something else was staring at him, drooling over his fat body.

The creature had an ugly face, distorted further by a wide grin stretching from one ear to the other. It was a witch—I could tell. Her unusually large eyes gleamed with gluttony. Her thin, grey hair clung loosely to her scrawny head. With each kiss, Sharma's energy seemed to drain away. When his hand moved further up, he realised, to his horror, that there was no body attached to the legs.

Instantly, he looked up—only to find a crooked head staring at him from the pillow.

Sharma froze as the head rose in the air, pushed by its neck, which kept elongating. Before Sharma could react, it dove into his flesh with the force of a cobra attacking its prey. Screams erupted in the night sky as I ran. I dropped from the window, my legs carrying me as fast as they could until I felt safe in the womb of my village.

The next day, the first policeman to emerge from the crime scene was retching uncontrollably. He announced, "Only a monster could do this. Seal this place!"

Ekant Sharma's wife was contacted the same day. She was in the city and had no clue about what had happened. Upon hearing the news of her husband, she went mad. She accused the rest of Ekant's family of bad blood and held the entire village accountable. A case was filed, but it went nowhere due to a lack of strong evidence.

I had always been a timid boy, easily frightened by darkness. This was far beyond anything my imagination could handle. I was too horrified to tell anyone what I had witnessed. I feared getting into trouble, and besides, who would believe me?

Sharma's little house was sealed with yellow tape that read 'Do not cross.' But one night, a storm swept all the tape away. On that very night, a couple from the city ventured into the house during their fun escapade. They were just getting comfortable when the man complained about seeing someone move across the house. He ignored it when the girl laughed at him for being a wuss.

They were facing each other, smiling, when the boy lifted his hands to remove his T-shirt, but as soon as it came off, the girl noticed that the back of his head was turned towards her. Assuming it to be some neat trick, she said, "Don't mess with me! Turn your face around."

Suddenly, the witch emerged from behind and said, "Let me help." She twisted his head, making it face the girl, breaking it in the process. The girl screamed in terror and ran. That night, wicked laughter echoed through the village, chilling the hearts of everyone who heard it.

The girl survived to tell the story. When her testimony confirmed the villagers' worst fears, everyone conjectured that the witch had taken up residence in Sharma's house due to the unresolved dispute. To prevent future incidents, they destroyed the cottage.

However, the matter was not laid to rest. One of the village pandits had an encounter that reignited the fear. One night, while returning from the city and making his way through the orchard, a sari fluttered down from a tree behind him. The pandit noticed it from the corner of his eye and immediately began chanting the powerful mantras of Lord Hanuman.

Suddenly, a voice teased him, "What you are reciting, Pandit, is meant for ghosts. I am just a lady." The voice crackled with sinister laughter before falling silent. Moments later, the witch emerged from his left, leering at him, only to disappear within seconds. Then, she reappeared from his right, hissing, "I want you." The pandit intensified his chanting, focusing all his energy on his lord, and managed to reach the village unharmed. He later recounted the event to a terrified crowd.

Countless other incidents followed, but none involved women. Villagers soon paved a new route to avoid the orchard altogether.

My father, who lived in the city, visited the village to handle some land-related work. Unaware of the stories about the orchard witch, he summoned me one evening to pick up his extra luggage from the bus stop outside the village. A few shops had sprung up near the bus stop, thanks to the regular hustle and bustle. Knowing my love for street food, he spent some time with me, indulging in the finest delicacies the place had to offer. Having met after so long, we lost track of time.

It was already dark by the time we started our journey back home. I kept warning my father about the orchard witch, but he thought I was making up stories. I refused to follow him on the orchard path, but he ignored my pleas. I was slapped for being adamant and ordered to follow him. All the joy from our evening had vanished in an instant. For a brief moment, I was angry at him, but left with no choice, I followed him onto the trail that led through the orchard.

Tears rolled down my cheeks as we approached the orchard. I remember carrying a small suitcase. When I heard her first whisper, my head instinctively turned towards the trees. I saw the witch hanging upside down from one of the branches, like a bat.

I forced myself to focus on the road, hoping the nightmare would end quickly. But a quick, furtive glance in her direction—and she was gone. I kept looking at the trees when suddenly, she moved past me.

"I remember you," she whispered, emerging from my left. "You're the same boy."

I shut my eyes tightly in utter dread and kept walking.

"Where are you taking your father?" she asked, shuffling towards my father's right.

That was it for me. I bolted. I heard my father shout my name, "Sunil! Sunil! Why are you running?"

But I ran with all my might. I saw her appear next to me as she mocked, "Yes, Sunil, why are you running? Are you leaving your father for me?"

When she said that, I stopped immediately, realising what she was about to do. I turned around and saw my father's feet trapped in a quagmire. He was crying for help, but I was so paralyzed with fear that I could barely move. I stood there, helpless, just like my father, watching as his body, piece by piece, began turning to stone until he was nothing but a statue.

I cannot forget her eyes when she called me out, cajoling, "Come, Sunil, don't you want to save your father?"

I carry this regret to this day. I could have done something then, but I didn't. I was weak. I ran home, terrified of her because I had seen what she was capable of. I was scared, wondering what she might do to me. But I am no longer afraid.

Back in the village, I told them what had happened, and they took immediate action. They torched the entire orchard. The statue was preserved like a piece of memorabilia to honour my father. A platform was built around it as a token of respect.

"After that incident, I moved to the city, knowing exactly what I had to do. With unwavering resolve, I delved into the world of dark arts, seeking out sages who practised black magic. That's when I met my Guru, Dagdu Pandit, who helped me conquer my fears. Under his guidance, I became a shaman, finally understanding the ways of the supernatural," Sunil revealed.

"You know, what's the most important thing?" Sunil looked up at the boy.

Aman was in complete awe. He shook his head.

"The most important thing is that I am no longer scared," answered Sunil.

The boy fidgeted, unnerved by the fierceness in the young man's eyes. Sunil held his hand to reassure him, "You don't need to be scared. Remember, it's fear that feeds her. Do not give her a chance!"

Aman felt Sunil's grip tighten around his wrist. He tried to pull away but couldn't. In that split second, he understood what was happening. His eyes darted up to something emerging from behind the statue. Everything Sunil had said was true. He was here for a reason. He was here for revenge.

For the first time, Aman beheld the face of the orchard witch. She was uglier than he had imagined—scarce hair clinging to her scalp, unusually large eyes, and the gaunt look of a creature that hadn't fed in a long time. She looked hungry. Aman couldn't stop screaming.

Before the witch could pounce on the little boy, Sunil spun around with a goblet and threw water on her face. It immediately began to burn, fumes erupting from her flesh. This time, the bellows of agony came from the witch as she covered her face with both hands, trying desperately to extinguish the flames.

Aman had fallen to the ground, watching in terror as the witch screeched in pain. Sunil was chanting mantra after mantra, his voice filled with unwavering resolve. He looked like a man on a mission—his eyes burning with vengeance. His voice thundered with the last mantra as he hurled the remaining water from the goblet, lancing the witch with the force of a whetted sword.

Amid a whirlpool of agony, the orchard witch exploded. Sparks of fire lit up the statue. Then silence returned as if nothing had happened.

A cracking noise echoed in the stillness. Sunil's glimmer of hope faded with the statue shattered, revealing a part of a skull. He knew it had been too long. There was no way his father could still be alive. When he reached out to touch the statue, it crumbled into dust.

"I am sorry, Father," he whispered under his breath.

The little boy was too stupefied to speak. He looked at Sunil and managed to ask, "Is she gone?"

Sunil picked up his bag to leave, turning to face the child one last time before concluding, "Yes, the nightmare is over."

# The Silhouette

"Yeah! That's the dare!" Kanika explained, excitement coursing through her veins.

"Oh! Do you think I'm scared?" Ananya challenged her assumption.

"Yes, you are," Shweta answered with a grin.

"I am not, okay?" Ananya snapped back immediately.

But deep down, Ananya was petrified, her thoughts consumed by the chilling prospect of stepping out into the corridor. Not only was she afraid of the darkness pooling under the dimly lit bulb near the staircase, but the thought of being left alone scared her even more. To make matters worse, her friends were daring her to take the entire trip by herself.

Every building in Mary Convent, an all-girls school, bore the weight of countless whispered tales. With a graveyard right next to the boundary wall, every student was convinced that the convent was haunted. Whispers of unnatural sightings at night always circulated through the dormitories. The girls loved thrilling nighttime stories, and ghost accounts were their second favourite pastime before bed. The first, of course, was the inevitable topic of boys.

Not long ago, a series of tragic suicides had shaken the very foundation of the convent. The incidents were kept under wraps, given how such matters tend to spiral out of control. The convent had a reputation to protect. The dilapidated old building was gradually undergoing renovation, and such rumours could only tarnish its name and undo the efforts to restore its glory.

Like every ruin that was once pristine and every fossil that was once alive, the convent, too, stood upon tales buried in its past. It secretly wished to lay its bricks anew and forget the rumours of the dead tarrying with the living. But just as a book is defined by its content rather than its cover, the fate of the convent rested in the hands of the children. It is always the posterity that holds the reins to either perpetuate or put an end to a legend.

With all this still fresh in the backdrop, some girls from the hostel were trying to provoke Ananya after seeing through her mask of feigned courage. They knew she was easily scared but wanted to have a little fun at her expense. What a dare!

"Okay, so let me get this straight," Ananya stood up, pretending to be enthusiastic.

"I have to exit from here," she pointed to the door, "then take a left from the stairs, pass through the corridor, and return from the back door," she pointed towards another door behind her, "thus completing the circle, right?"

"Yes!" everyone shouted in unison. The excitement of the adventure was killing them.

"Okay, done!" Ananya agreed.

A thick silence settled. Ananya took a deep breath, mentally clocking the impending event and picturing how she would carry out the task. She glanced at the clock—2 AM, the Devil's Hour!

*"Why didn't I sleep early today?"*

The other girls, the audience, waited impatiently on their beds, eyes peeled open. Some even had their blankets ready, half-covering their faces. It was both thrilling and unsettling. The mere thought of a solo walk down the corridor in the dead of night was crazy enough to give them chills.

Goosebumps rose as they watched Ananya step out slowly, her steps unsure. The dim light from the staircase cast only a silhouette of her figure as she moved forward. After taking a few steps, she abruptly stopped. Everyone's eyes remained glued to her.

Her silhouette stood motionless in the darkness ahead. The girls in the room exchanged anxious glances, their eyes wide with astonishment, before shifting their gaze back to the still figure.

"Guys! Why isn't Ananya moving?" one of them finally broke the silence.

"I don't know. Has she seen something?" Kanika wondered aloud.

Shweta even called out her name to make her turn, but the silhouette didn't budge.

"Was this a bad idea?" a girl lamented.

"We should never have asked her to go. That was stupid," Shweta added, her voice filled with regret.

"Kanika, go check on her!" Seema ordered.

"Why should I go? You sent her! You go!" Kanika protested, already terrified.

"Shweta, let's go together," Seema suggested, but Shweta was quick to refuse.

Everyone waited, their pulses racing. Despite their hushed debate, nobody dared move. All eyes remained fixated on the silhouette when, out of nowhere, Ananya returned from the back door and announced, "Guys! I did it."

Shrieks of horror filled the room as everyone turned back to check the silhouette—it had disappeared.

A puzzled Ananya looked around, trying to understand why her friends seemed so shaken. When they filled her in about the mysterious silhouette, Ananya was utterly baffled. She had found the journey uneventful, and although she had been scared of the dare, she had still completed it without any incident. Shweta quickly closed the door and jumped back onto her bed.

Everyone tried to sleep that night, but they failed miserably. Even though the silhouette had vanished, the haunting image of it standing there, utterly still, doing absolutely nothing, refused to leave their minds.

# River of Charon

Through distant echoes in the unknown corridors of my mind, I felt myself gradually dissolving into reality. As my subconscious parted ways with my final thought, my eyelids flickered—slow at first, then snapping open abruptly. Yet, it felt as if my eyes hadn't opened at all, for the world outside was the same colour. Pitch-black. Only, it was darker than my dream.

As my eyes adjusted to the darkness, I sat up at once and peered into the night, trying to see what was around me—what had possibly consumed me. Rocks. Rocks everywhere. The scent of damp earth hit my nose.

*"Water!"* There was water nearby. If one listened closely, the faint sound of ripples could be heard.

*"Why is it so dark in here? Where am I?"*

I felt stones on my palm. I picked one up and threw it in front of me. A tiny blast of water rose briefly before disappearing as if nothing had happened. I picked up another one and threw it to my right, aiming at the darkness. A familiar fountain rose before vanishing into the void. Next, I threw one to my left. It struck something solid, producing a hollow sound that disrupted the silence with its echo.

A droplet of sweat trickled down my neck as I realised what I had just hit. It was a skull.

I scanned my surroundings. I hadn't been throwing stones—I had woken up on a pile of bones. I was someone's fodder.

I stood up at once, my eyes dilated, and tried to walk. Bones beneath me crackled under my weight. I looked up, searching for anything I could make out, but the night stared back at me.

*"What is this place? How did I end up here?"*

Within a few seconds, I understood there was nowhere to go. I moved forward and shouted in despair, "Hello! Hello! Is anybody here?"

Then I waited for something to respond—anything, other than my echo, which reverberated from all directions. Driven by disquiet and curiosity, I wandered around helplessly before my legs felt the cold, tingling touch of water. With nowhere else to go, I returned to where I had started.

I sat there alone in the darkness, surrounded by my island of thoughts, waiting for something to happen.

I couldn't remember where I had been. I couldn't even remember going to bed.

*"Is this a dream?"*

I pinched myself to check, only to feel the sting of regret.

As I cursed aloud at my folly for pinching myself like a child, something caught my attention. A glint of light struck me from a distant point in the darkness. In its dim reflection, I saw the shape of an oar rise and fall, carefully pushing back the river as if not to disturb the stillness of the water. It seemed to be heading directly towards me.

I stood up at once, frantically waving my arms.

"Hello! Hello! Help! I'm here!"

But there was no deviation in the rhythm of the oar. It rose and fell at its own steady pace. I watched the ripples caused by the oar silently approaching me, carrying a message I couldn't yet decipher.

Whoever manned the boat was unfazed by the urgency in my voice. For a second, I doubted if my cries could even reach him. The only good news was that the boat was indeed coming towards me.

"Yes! Yes! Please! Thank you so much!"

Relief began to wash over me.

*"Finally, I'll be able to get the hell out of here."*

But when the boat came a little closer, I was taken aback by what I saw. A towering figure manned the oar. His face was hidden beneath a hood, and his robes were no darker than the night itself. He wore silence-like mourning robes, and his boat—a hearse—whispered, *"Your time has come."*

Suddenly, it dawned on me. It was the Ferryman who had come to take me. The slap of the cold, heartless Styx against my legs confirmed my worst fear—I was dead.

I felt the claws of despondency pricking me from within. A tear rolled down my cheek as I fell to my knees. A life unlived made a vague attempt to beckon me, but I couldn't remember any of the faces.

*"There was so much to do. So many things to try, so many unfinished dreams."*

Regret began piling up in my mind as the formidable ferry hit the shore. Its keel crushed the bones beneath it as it made its way towards the land. The Ferryman lifted his oar.

With tears blurring my vision, I tried to catch a glimpse of his face—if only it were there. Nothing but darkness stared back at me from his hood. That giant remained unmoved, his hood concealing any trace of a face as if waiting for me to board. I took a deep breath, picked myself up, and climbed into the boat.

The rhythmic rowing resumed as the boat drifted forward. I was crying profusely now, snivelling with every faceless memory that haunted me. I clasped my head with both hands and wept, struggling to remember the life I had lived.

I could recall the moments I had experienced, but couldn't remember who I had shared them with. Even a faceless dog appeared in my memory, but when I tried to hold onto it, its features dissolved like mist.

I was sifting through broken fragments of my past when I noticed the silence—the rowing had stopped. Assuming we had reached our destination,

I braced myself to alight. But then, I felt a nudge of the oar against my back. I turned around to see the Ferryman, his hand raised towards me as if imploring me to give him something.

Suddenly, it struck me. *"Ah! The toll! He wants a coin."*

I started searching my pockets, but they seemed empty at first. I scoured them again, more carefully this time, wondering if I had missed a corner.

Meanwhile, the Ferryman stood motionless, his hand still outstretched.

I continued to check my other pockets more painstakingly, weighed down by the gnawing thought at the back of my mind—*what would happen if I couldn't pay Charon's toll?*

Nothing. I had nothing on me. I pretended to scavenge again, desperately hoping to find something, but I came up empty-handed every time.

*"This is so important. How do I not even have a dime on me?"*

The dark figure stared at me as I managed a meek reply, "I'm sorry... I don't have anything to give to you."

With that, his hand slowly lowered. An uneasy silence followed. I tried to break it by asking, "Am I still allowed to go?"

But the Ferryman didn't reply. He stood there, motionless.

I was about to speak again, but was cut off by a scuffle in the waters—something stirring beneath the surface. A bubbling sound rose behind me, followed by a gurgling one to my left. Soon, it was all around me, as if my audacity had awakened demons from the netherworld.

I saw that we were close to a patch of land on my right.

*"Probably the place where I was being taken."*

I decided to dash for it before things could worsen. But before I could jump, I felt Charon's mighty oar strike me on the head. I plunged into the icy waters of the Styx.

Within seconds, a dozen hands were on me. I felt gnawing teeth sink into my skin. I bellowed in pain, but only bubbles escaped my mouth as I realised I was being dragged down.

The pain was unbearable. I could feel unseen creatures tearing away my flesh. The sensation of having your skin ripped from your body numbs you after a while, but it was all new to me. I had never experienced the horror of 'being eaten alive.'

Whether it was my instinct or desperation that kicked in, I managed to land blows on the predator,s pushing them away with whatever strength I had left. I surfaced, gasping for breath, only to realise I had drifted away from the ferry. With my destination only a few dives away, I started swimming as hard as I could towards the land. As I cut through the numbing water, I felt myself getting closer.

*"I'll make a run for it once I'm on land. Then I'll be safe."*

The sound of chattering teeth behind me grew louder with every stroke. Occasionally, they came so close that they brushed against my feet, but I was nimble enough to evade them.

I kept going until my knees scraped against the riverbed. I scrambled onto land, refusing to look back. Celebrating my small victory, I collapsed to my knees. As I hit the ground, a familiar crackling noise echoed beneath me. A shimmer of light illuminated what I had crushed—and I realised, to my horror, that I had trudged onto bones once again.

I turned around to see the faint glow of light coming from the distant ferry. I was back where I had started—in the land of the dead. I ran my hands over my body. Blood seeped from countless punctures, and loose flesh hung from me like frayed bandages.

I lay motionless on the pile of bones beneath me, laughing like a lunatic until I felt I was about to pass out. For the first time, the darkness around me seemed to grow even darker.

# THE CURSE OF ARIPA

People often wonder, "*Why is Aripa cursed? Why does the sun never shine in Aripa?*" Last year, Aripa recorded around 26,000 millimetres of rainfall—the highest amount ever received by any place on the planet. Scientists claim it's a geographical phenomenon, but if you listen to the stories told by the people from the nearby town, an entirely different folktale emerges.

Back in the days when the village had yet to embrace technology, Arth, a 13-year-old boy, and a group of his friends went to play in the woods next to the village. Almost every teenager in the village was there, including Shabd, his 10-year-old younger brother, who always tagged along wherever Arth went.

Everyone agreed to play hide-and-seek. It was Arth's turn to be the seeker. Titters erupted as he stepped into the heart of the forest, trying to find the rest of his gang—a task made difficult since everyone had become adept at hiding.

Shabd was a reckless hider, and Arth expected to find him first. However, when a nearby bush shook, his short-lived excitement faded as he discovered it was just a rabbit darting down the trail.

Right after, there was a splashing noise, as if someone had jumped into marshy water. Arth ran frantically towards the sound, only to stop short before the soggy ground. In the quagmire ahead, he saw a hand sinking into the swamp. It shook helplessly, trying to find something to hold on to.

Arth's heart nearly stopped when he discovered that it was none other than his brother's hand. A small tattoo of Ganesha was imprinted on the wrist, just like the one on Shabd's hand. Screaming his name in agony, Arth tried to step into the marsh but retreated when it began to consume him as well. Helplessly, he circled the bog, shouting Shabd's name at the top of his lungs, alerting his friends who were still in hiding.

Amid the chaos and confusion, Arth's eyes fell on a long, broken branch. He quickly flung one end towards the slowly disappearing hand. When Shabd's fingers felt it, they grabbed the branch and tugged hard. The force was so intense that it uprooted Arth's feet, yanking him towards the bog.

The rest of the cavalry arrived.

"What happened?" they shouted almost in unison.

"Shabd! That's Shabd!" Arth could barely manage, gasping for breath.

"What are you talking about?" Shabd called out from behind.

Utter terror painted Arth's face as he tried to connect the dots. Shabd had been with the rest of the gang all along. Marred by disbelief, he looked back at the quagmire. There was no hand there, only the stick he was holding. Yet, it was still being pulled by something beneath the marsh. With another powerful tug, Arth let go at once.

Back in the village, Arth was shaking to the core as he struggled to narrate the entire account to a group of villagers. His trembling didn't subside, not even when the village pundit tried to calm him down. Upon hearing the story, the pundit took a deep breath and said, "I thought it was just a tale, but after what happened in the woods today, there's a chance it might be true."

He faced the baffled crowd before continuing, "Aripa used to be a bountiful land before it was cursed."

Met with raised eyebrows, the pundit elaborated further, "I know it's hard to believe, but this land carries the burden of a blemished past. Our sacred grounds were once pillaged by plunderers. They would descend out of nowhere and seize everything left in the open. People would bolt their doors, leaving those outside to their fate."

The crowd had gradually swelled around the pundit. After taking another deep breath, he resumed, "A girl from Chaneri, our nearby village, had come to visit Aripa on one such unfortunate day. Unaware of the danger, she was left exposed."

Gasps of commiseration filled the air as the villagers absorbed the plight of the poor girl.

The story continued, "She banged on every door in the village, but no one opened. Chased by the wicked claws of leering men, she ran towards a swampy pond that used to lie at the centre of the village."

The pundit pointed towards an open area near the village well. "To save herself from the filthy robbers, she rushed straight to the heart of it and drowned."

"Not a single door opened. Yet a thousand helpless eyes watched her being consumed by the bog from the cracks in their windows."

Silence prevailed when the pundit finished the tale. The villagers stood, ashamed of the deeds of their ancestors. Radheshwar, the village Sarpanch, broke the silence. "Look around you. Why do you think Aripa receives rainfall every day?"

Binesh, a farmer, shouted, "Aren't we living under her curse?"

Arth chimed in, "We are being punished for the deeds of our forefathers."

Shabd joined in too, "There are puddles and swamps everywhere."

The pundit tried to conclude, "We are living in a mire of our own making. Yes."

Sarita, a widow, sobbed, "The village has seen enough tragedies already. Too many people have died by drowning."

Someone from the crowd shouted, "She is hunting us."

Another added, "It's vengeance!"

Everyone's blood curdled as they voiced their fears and resentment, one after another.

Arth looked at the pundit and asked, "What's the solution?

Everyone waited with bated breath. The pundit met Arth's gaze and said, "Our village needs vindication. We will perform a grand *Yajna*—a fire ritual—at the heart of the village, the very spot where she presumably died."

"Will it work?" Radheshwar asked.

The pundit glanced at him and replied, "We can only hope her restless soul finds peace with our offering and leave the rest to God."

The next day, Aripa woke up to the sound of conch shells. As usual, the sky was shrouded in clouds. Incantations followed under a huge shed to protect against the rain. Spells and chants that no one had ever heard before resonated through the village. The villagers gathered all around the fire pit, their curiosity piqued like children drawn to something mysterious. No one had ever seen a ritual as grand as the one being performed by the pundit. Everyone knew the reason behind it. No one dared question him.

The ritual sprawled into the evening. Devotees slowly returned to their homes, satisfied with the offerings. Everyone was hopeful that the pundit had done his best to rid the village of evil once and for all.

The next morning, a miracle occurred—one that the villagers had never witnessed before. When Arth pulled back his curtains, a streak of sunlight streamed into his room. He rushed outside to find the villagers dancing with joy. The sun beamed down upon them, and not a single cloud marred the sky.

"Finally, the curse has been lifted!" Radheshwar bellowed at the top of his lungs.

"She's gone!" Binesh cheered, dancing with his goat.

"The pundit has done it!" someone from the crowd shouted.

Euphoria swept through the village. Many carried their chairs and beds outside to bask in the long-lost sunlight. It felt as though Aripa had been reborn. The day was immediately declared a festival, and the village sculptor began working on a statue to commemorate the occasion. The drunkards started drinking as early as the afternoon.

The pundit became an overnight hero. Bags of wheat and rice were sent to his house as a token of gratitude. Despite being lifted onto shoulders and urged to dance, he tried to remain humble.

The entire day was a celebration. Nobody went to work, and the village school was closed so the children could partake in the revelry. Hips swayed to the thunderous beat of the drums. The savoury aroma of mutton and chicken wafted through the air. Food and drinks were dispatched to neighbouring villages as a gesture of goodwill.

People partied until nightfall, eventually gathering around a huge bonfire where even the sceptics found themselves converted into believers.

As the night wore on, everyone retired after enjoying the finest meal of their lives. Many complained of cramped necks, hips, and legs from all the dancing. Soon, Aripa snored away, lost in a haze of booze and smoke.

Late at night, Arth awoke with a parched throat. As he stirred, he heard a strange noise in the background. Too tired to care, he reached for his pot of water. The water level was low, so he dipped his hand in to scoop it out with a cup. But as he tried to withdraw his hand, he realised it was stuck.

*"Did my hand grow, or did the pot's opening somehow shrink?"*

He tugged hard, but his hand wouldn't budge. He even tried lifting the pot, but it had become unusually heavy. Just then, his window burst open. A storm raged outside. A flash of lightning illuminated the silhouette of a girl standing at the heart of the village, where the rituals had been performed. The area was now submerged in water, and she stood motionless in the middle of the pool.

Suddenly, something cold brushed against Arth's stuck hand. When he looked at the pot, he was horrified to see it brimming with bog. The swamp inside was pulling him in. He yanked his hand, screaming as he tugged desperately, only to wake up, gasping for breath.

It was just a nightmare.

Relief washed over him as he sat upright on his bed, his throat still parched. Squinting at the pot before him, he ignored his thirst and lay back down.

But then, he realised something—the familiar pitter-patter sound from his dream hadn't stopped. It continued in the background, growing louder.

Arth sprang out of bed, only to land in a puddle. His floor had transformed into a mire. Water was everywhere. His family was nowhere to be found. He scrambled towards the door, but it wouldn't budge. He shouted for help, but the only reply he received was the anguished cries of other villagers trapped inside their homes.

That night, Aripa was wiped off the face of the earth. The land recorded its highest rainfall ever, and the mire swallowed every remaining trace of the village.

Not a soul survived.

# The Haunting of Saraidih

Saraidih, a village in Palamu, Jharkhand, harbours its share of secrets. Only the locals understand the true terrors of being a Saraidihan. To begin with, the village has resigned itself to the constant threat of Naxalite plundering. Villagers carry guns wherever they go, always prepared for any kind of unforeseen attack.

Saraidih, being very close to the forest, also experiences frequent animal attacks. Then, there are the stories—tales of ghosts and demons lurking in the shadows at various corners of the village. Ask anyone, and they'll have their own supernatural account to narrate. These ghastly sightings have embedded themselves into the heart of the village's lore. To an outsider, all of this might seem a bit unusual, but to the villagers, it has become a way of life.

Jeet, a 24-year-old man, lived in a nearby village called Namudag. After having an early dinner, he headed to his roof to sleep. He was about to drift into a deep slumber when the piercing sound of an engine purring into the night woke him up.

His friends, Dhakku and Varg, from Saraidih, were on a motorcycle, calling him out to visit a funfair in their village. Festive events were always spectacular in Saraidih, and Jeet couldn't miss it for the world. Within a few minutes, they were riding triple on the main road that led to Saraidih. Even though the villages were almost 5 kilometres apart, it hardly took them 10 minutes to reach.

The festive occasion was a huge hit among the locals. People danced to the beats of the latest songs. Even when there wasn't a performance, one could see kids dancing behind the stage area. Firecrackers lit up the sky during performance breaks, leaving the audience awestruck. Soon, hilarious plays were staged, and everyone guffawed, holding their bellies. Some were driven to the edge of their seats when a magician began to perform impossible tricks. Overall, it was a befitting night worth remembering—far from the usual routine in Namudag, and for that, Jeet was deeply grateful.

It had been two hours since his arrival when Jeet realised it was getting late. He excused himself, letting Dhakku and Varg know that he planned to head home before midnight. Jeet had already started walking when Varg ran up to him with a pistol.

"This is for your safety," he winked as he slipped it into Jeet's hand.

Jeet knew what it meant to travel alone at night and welcomed the aid. He set out for Namudag around 11 PM. On a moonlit night of undeniable clarity, he walked alone along a trail that would eventually connect to a thoroughfare ahead.

Open fields stretched on either side as Jeet walked. Trees stood guard at the edges, with large bushes lining the trail at every step. The chirping of crickets was so familiar that it had blended into the rhythm of his nights. Jeet found their sounds amusing as they filled the air with a soothing melody, far removed from Saraidih's triumphant festivities, which had faded with each step he took away from the village. A few more steps and every noise would vanish, lost in the far reaches of the galaxy, merging into the fabric of white noise.

When Jeet began to feel tired, he noticed a figure walking on the trail ahead. Somewhere in the recesses of his subconscious, he imagined the man had emerged from the left side of the field, only to vanish and reappear on the right, now waiting at the graveyard near the next turn.

While Jeet was still busy contemplating the idea of having some company on his way back home, he failed to realise that the man had already started walking beside him.

"Where are you headed?" asked the curious stranger, trying to match Jeet's pace.

Startled by the man's sudden emergence, Jeet tried to remain calm and replied, "Home."

"Why don't you come to Birhordih with me?" the stranger suggested, his tone oddly insistent.

Jeet knew Birhordih was another nearby village, but taking that route would lead him off his intended path.

"Why would I want to go there?" Jeet replied calmly, trying to ease the tension building up in his head.

"C'mon, it's not that far," entreated the stranger.

"But why would I want to go there?" Jeet countered once again.

"It's very close," the stranger urged.

"My home is this way," Jeet pointed in the direction he had been headed all along.

Carefully aware of how insistently the stranger was trying to lead him down a different path, Jeet maintained his composure. Yet, the stranger persisted, "Come, let's go!"

A huge tree cast a shadow across the trail. As they began crossing it, Jeet saw for the first time who he had been conversing with. In the shade of the tree, the stranger had completely disappeared, only to reappear under the moonlight. His profile seemed to have gradually materialised from the mist.

Jeet noticed that the thoroughfare he was heading towards was just ahead. He quickly leapt onto it, stepping onto the rough concrete gravel of the main road before turning around to check on the stranger. The latter had stopped on the trail itself.

The entity gnashed its teeth angrily and threatened, "If I see you on this path again, I will kill you."

That chilling voice sent a wave of dread through Jeet. Instinctively, he reached for the pistol. The stranger grew into a humongous size, almost matching the tree's dimensions. At that moment, Jeet pulled the trigger.

Three gunshots echoed through the night, one after the other, shattering the silence. Creatures in the trees and bushes stirred from their disrupted slumber, murmuring their displeasure before settling back into the prevailing silence. The demon stood motionless for a moment before fading and disappearing into the darkness of the tree.

Scampering with whatever courage remained, Jeet sprinted the rest of the way home. Along the way, he glanced over his shoulder multiple times, fearful of being followed. Only when the warm glow of the lights from his hometown touched him did he finally stop and take a deep breath.

The next morning, when Jeet tried to recount the events of the night to his family, no one believed him. Later, when Dhakku and Varg came to visit, the three of them decided to return to the spot where the incident had occurred.

Upon reaching the site, they discovered three bullet holes embedded in the bark of the tree where the demon had last been seen.

# THE FOLKLORE OF CHHAYAPUR

Many people from rural India used to defecate in the fields. In many regions, this practice is still considered a socially accepted way of life. Only those accustomed to city life complain about it, but due to a lack of choice, they too are sometimes seen squatting in the fields.

Chhayapur, a small village situated near the banks of the River Ganga, was no exception to this unvoiced convention. Women were the first to wake up in the morning for their daily chores, which always began with a trip to the fields. In Chhayapur, there was an unspoken understanding between men and women—an ingrained sense of humility that consistently placed women first.

Beyond physical hardship, the people of Chhayapur exhibited mental regression as well, which was evident time and again. When Binita had a baby, her in-laws refused to accept it because it was a girl. The newborn was cast into the river, discarded like unwanted waste, joining the persistent societal decay. No mortal could tell whether the river had wept alongside Binita on that unfortunate day.

Binita was a 20-year-old girl from the city, married to Vikram, a 25-year-old mechanic who owned a shop on the outskirts of the village. He was usually out during the daytime. Vikram's family were farmers who owned various patches of land scattered across Chhayapur.

In the beginning, Binita had a hard time adjusting to the ways of the village. However, she soon became conditioned by the way everyone lived. Since it was a large family, she spent most of her time in the kitchen, cooking for everyone after cleaning the house. Then, she had to wash their clothes, pin them to hangers, bring them back in the evening, and fold them for everyone. Cleaning utensils right after a meal and then prepping for the next one even consumed her siesta time.

Even after doing so much, her mother-in-law would often be heard complaining about petty things. But a city girl could only take so much.

When Binita's baby was murdered, she remained an emotional wreck for months. She stopped eating properly and began questioning the meaning of her existence. Binita often had nightmares about her dead child. She spent days wondering—had the child been allowed to live, she would have grown into a beautiful little girl.

Binita blamed herself for being heartless enough to allow such a thing to happen in the first place. Someone had snatched a living, breathing soul that she had carried and nurtured for nine months in her womb. How could she let them take her baby away? Why didn't Vikram say a word?

Moving on doesn't happen in a day, but with ample time and other things to worry about, the dead are eventually forgotten. Time, being the most powerful element in the universe, won yet another war when it forced her to let go of the grief she had been holding on to for so long.

One fine day, Binita woke up a little later than usual and headed straight for the fields. There was no time to waste, as daybreak was about to happen. If she had woken up Brinda, her neighbour and friend, to go with her, it would have already been too late.

Binita liked to relieve herself near the field by the river because of its easy accessibility. The spot she chose overlooked the river. She went further into the bushes to avoid being noticed by any early risers.

It was still dark, but the clouds near the horizon carried the first hint of an impending sunrise. Restless birds in the trees could be heard gearing up for another routine. Tall grasses rustled as they brushed against each other. It was going to be a windy day after all.

As Binita was about to get up, she felt something tugging at one loose end of her sari. When she turned around to check, she almost shrieked.

It was hard to tell what it was. It looked unearthly, like some kind of small animal with big human eyes. The grotesque creature had large, pointy ears that twitched at every sound. Its body was covered with hair. There was something about those enchanting eyes that stopped Binita from running away. They were bright blue eyes that seemed to beseech her to stay.

"What are you?" an awestruck Binita whispered.

Suddenly, the creature started whimpering like a baby. It toddled towards her as if seeking comfort. She could tell the creature pined for love. Instead of warding it off, Binita slowly lifted her hand as if to beckon it. Just as she was about to do that, a nearby bird flapped its wings, startling the creature. The noise sent it scuttling away towards the river, disappearing within seconds.

Binita sat there in silence, processing what she had seen.

"What was that? Am I dreaming?"

When she returned to her household chores, she couldn't stop thinking about what she had witnessed.

"It wasn't an animal."

She tried to tell Vikram, but he laughed it off. "It must have been a rabbit or a dog," he said.

"It didn't look like an animal," she insisted, tossing restlessly in bed. She couldn't sleep that night.

The thought of revisiting that place alone unsettled her, so she decided to take Brinda with her the next day. She snuck out early in the morning, insisting that a yawning Brinda join her. On the way, she tried to explain the urgency, but like Vikram, Brinda also had her fair share of laughs.

They visited the same field overlooking the river. Brinda kept talking in the background, going on and on about her in-laws, but Binita barely paid attention. Her eyes constantly wandered towards the river, but nothing appeared. Even after they were done, Binita insisted on staying for a while. They waited until sunrise before finally returning. Binita was disappointed that the magical creature hadn't shown up.

The next few days were no different—no sign of the creature anywhere. This went on until Binita began to question whether she had seen anything at all.

"Maybe I was hallucinating."

During their morning trips, Binita often asked Brinda about the village. Brinda was a tattletale, always eager to share stories. What surprised Binita the most was that every villager of Chhayapur harboured a blunt disregard for women. It was a brazenly patriarchal society that didn't allow them to have a voice.

One morning, Binita woke up and decided not to take Brinda with her. She had been toying with the idea for a while. Maybe it was Brinda's presence that kept the creature from revealing itself.

Binita waited near the river, tracing the shore before getting on with her daily chores. She lingered at the banks, gazing at the sunrise, but once again, she was met with disappointment. That day, she stayed out longer than usual. When she finally returned home, she was scolded by her mother-in-law. The house was already bustling, and everyone was waiting for their early morning tea.

Something in Binita snapped that day when she retorted at her in-laws' comments.

"What's so hard about making tea for yourselves?" Binita almost shouted.

"Why can't anybody do anything in this house on their own?"

Everyone in the family was stumped. It was so unlike her. Binita had been carrying her frustration for so long that it had finally erupted. She was tired of being the one who was always at the receiving end.

When Binita went inside and shut the door behind her, Vikram's mother asked, "Is she all right?"

After crying her eyes out, Binita emerged in the afternoon and resumed her household chores, feeling a little guilty. Yet, at the same time, she was relieved for having said what needed to be said. It was about time she set some boundaries.

The result was positive—everyone was extra polite to her that day. They seemed careful around her. However, things are often different behind closed doors. Vikram gave her a tough time later, arguing about the way she had spoken to his mother.

"Chhayapur isn't used to voices," Vikram stated. "It has always been like that around here."

"But Vikram, haven't I done enough for this family?" Binita questioned, her voice trembling.

"For a family, nothing is ever enough. You have to listen to their needs and comply, no matter what," Vikram asserted.

"You cannot complain about any injustice. If you have something on your mind, you can talk to me here, in bed. What you did was unacceptable!"

Vikram ended the conversation with a teary-eyed Binita, who could barely speak in her defence.

As the whole house snored, Binita could think only of the injustices she had endured. Vikram's stand that night had made her feel like a prisoner in her own home.

"Everybody needs me here, but what about my needs? Why does nobody ask me what I want?"

The next day, Binita found herself sitting in the same field, lost in thought. She had almost given up on the idea of the creature when, out of the blue, it appeared before her again.

Whimpering like a child, it gradually hopped towards her. For a moment, Binita wondered if it was just a rabbit, but as she looked closer, her doubts faded.

Unlike a rabbit's ears, its ears were positioned where human ears are. Its bright blue eyes shone even brighter that day—big, beautiful eyes that seemed to understand her pain. Its face was hairless and innocent, but the rest of its body was fully covered in fur. Where there should have been hands, there were none—just limbs without paws. With no tail, it toddled on all fours, occasionally sitting on its rump.

"It is a baby!" Binita almost screamed with joy.

This time, Binita let the creature come closer, careful not to make any sudden movements. She beckoned it by shaking a leaf gently. When the baby came near, Binita lifted her hand and stroked its head. It chortled softly at her gentle touch, filling her heart with such joy that tears welled in her eyes.

Convinced that it was her child visiting her from beyond the grave, Binita lifted the creature and immediately wrapped it in the loose end of her sari. Then, she hurried towards home.

It was still dark when she quietly slipped into an abandoned corner of the house and entered the storage room. There, she carefully unwrapped her sari to reveal the endearing, hairy child with big, pointy ears. It still seemed happy to be around her.

"I will call you Chhaya," Binita whispered. The baby cackled as Binita shushed her, then quickly poured some milk into a bowl and offered it. Chhaya immediately started slurping—she seemed hungry.

Binita locked the storage room door and began her day in a playful mood. She was singing as she made tea for everyone. People noticed her happiness and tried to recall the last time they had seen her like that.

When Binita was in the kitchen, Brinda dropped by for a bowl of rice. Some jovial comments followed, and laughter filled the air. The atmosphere was one of promise, merriment, and hope.

When the noise died, Binita heard her mother-in-law ask Brinda to fetch rice from the storeroom. Binita nearly jumped out of her skin when she heard that. She dropped the utensil in her hand and ran towards the room, but she was too late. Brinda had already opened the door and stepped inside.

Terrified shrieks echoed through every nook and cranny of the house as Brinda ran out, shouting, "Demon! Demon! There's a demon inside!"

Binita froze when she saw Vikram heading towards the storeroom to check. However, he came out moments later and said, "What is wrong with you, Brinda? There's nothing inside."

"Yes, there is! It has big teeth and pointy ears!" Brinda insisted, shuddering with dread as she struggled to recall the vague features of the creature she had seen.

Surprised at Vikram's response, Binita ran into the room. She came out confused, confirming that Vikram was right—there was no one inside.

"Where did Chhaya go?"

Brinda tried to explain once more, when someone mocked her, saying she might have seen herself in the mirror. The rest of the family joined in, adding to the barrage of jibes. Poor Brinda, she couldn't explain what she had seen without being made fun of. The same people who had been friendly and kind to her just minutes ago were now jeering and laughing at her. Brinda looked at Binita helplessly before walking away.

Binita spent the whole day looking for Chhaya, but the baby was nowhere to be found. What stood out was the fact that there was no window in the storeroom.

"How could Chhaya escape? If she's still in the house, where did she go?" Binita wondered before deciding to check on Brinda.

Brinda was a wreck. When she described what she had seen in the storeroom, Binita began to doubt whether it was the same creature. Brinda's description painted a picture of some kind of monstrous being.

As Binita got up to leave, Brinda grabbed her hand and said, "You were right about seeing something near the river. I think I saw it today at your house. I know what you were trying to tell me the other day. I understand what it feels like to be unheard, to not have a voice. I know now."

Binita didn't say a word. She returned, hoping to find Chhaya still in the house. She searched discreetly through the rooms, but there was no sign of her that day.

That night, when Binita tried to talk about the incident, Vikram dismissed her, saying that Brinda had always been crazy.

"What if she was right?" Binita tried to defend her friend.

"Then the monster is already here. God save us," Vikram said mockingly, deriding the idea.

Binita replayed in her mind the reaction she would get if she told Vikram everything—everything about her secret little monster. But there was no way he would believe her. Fighting every urge to stay silent, she decided to confess.

"I might have brought something into the house."

She waited patiently for Vikram's reply, but he was already asleep. His snores made her realise how pointless the conversation would have been.

That night, Binita had the deepest slumber of her life. She remembered waking up at one point and realising that she was breastfeeding Chhaya. Binita smiled at her. But when the baby smiled back, its mouth opened wide, revealing huge, sharp teeth. Loose flesh hung casually from them. The gaping maw made it clear that Chhaya wasn't feeding on milk, but on Binita's very blood.

It wasn't the nightmare that woke Binita, but the sound of wailing. Someone had died in the neighbourhood. When she found out it was none other than Brinda, she was paralyzed with shock.

As she stepped outside, she heard whispers about the gruesome scene—there was blood everywhere. No one could determine what had happened. Some suspected an animal attack, while others speculated it was a cold-blooded murder, noting that the marks on Brinda's body were unlike any animal bite.

The whole atmosphere had turned sombre. Brinda's family wept, and Binita and her family stood by their side at every step. The constant wailing struck Binita's conscience like a funeral knell. Deep down, she felt responsible.

That day, she went near the river and screamed into the void. She ranted, cursing her wretched fate and her poor decisions. Her voice startled a few birds, while some onlookers watched in confusion, failing to understand what had driven her to madness.

When she returned home that night, resuming life as usual was no easy task. But what surprised her most was how the rest of the household carried on as if nothing had happened.

Just then, someone went as far as to mock Brinda's face when she visited the storeroom. Others sniggered at the stupid joke. That was it for Binita. She lost her cool once again and shouted, "What is wrong with you? Where is your decency?"

In a fit of rage, she threw her plate and continued, "All this time, I was blaming myself. But it's not just me—it's all of you. Each one of you is equally responsible. You mocked her when she was alive, and now you mock her in death. Do you have no sense of shame?"

Everyone gawked at her in disbelief. Her mother-in-law whispered something under her breath. Binita stomped away, declaring, "I cannot be a part of this place. This house is a disgrace."

That same night, Binita fought with Vikram when he tried to calm her down. He was justifying their wrongs, which only infuriated her further. The entire house heard their heated argument before Binita slammed the door behind her, yelling, "Everyone here is crazy. I cannot live here anymore."

With tears in her eyes, she headed towards the river. She chose a tree she often visited and sat beneath it, crying.

A rustle in the bushes made her look up, and she saw Chhaya toddling towards her. She still had the same innocent, bright blue eyes as when Binita had first met her. There was no trace of fear in the baby anymore as she walked straight into Binita's lap.

"Hey! There you are. Where have you been?" Binita murmured, caressing Chhaya as she purred, brushing her head affectionately against Binita.

"I thought I had brought you home," Binita continued. "But then you..." Suddenly, she remembered Brinda's death.

"Did you have anything to do with it?" Binita asked hesitantly. The baby only gazed at her, purring occasionally when stroked on the head.

"How could you hurt anybody? Look at those eyes," Binita whispered, shaking off the thought. Chhaya snuggled closer, settling comfortably in her lap.

It had been a long and exhausting day for Binita. Her eyes grew heavy. The baby tugged at the loose end of her sari as if asking her to take it along once again.

"I don't want to go back to that place anymore. Everyone there is a monster," Binita muttered, glancing in the direction of the village. The baby made a soft cooing noise. Just then, two or three more creatures like Chhaya emerged, toddling towards Binita.

"Oh, there are more like you." Binita was surprised at first, but then she smiled softly. Exhaustion overtook her, and she slipped into an inevitable slumber. The last thing she saw was Chhaya's companions hopping and toddling towards her.

When Binita woke up, she realised she had fallen asleep under the tree. The sun was up. Faint memories resurfaced as she looked around, searching for Chhaya.

*"Was that a dream?"*

Shaking off that thought, she hurried home. On her way back, her mind replayed the terrible fight with Vikram, and guilt gnawed her. She regretted how things had ended the previous night.

"Vikram must still be furious. It'll take more than just words—perhaps his favourite desserts—to calm him down," she thought. She resolved to apologize to everyone, explaining that Brinda's death had shaken her. The day had been unbearable, and she had simply lost control.

But when Binita stepped into the house and reached the threshold of her room, she froze in dazed disbelief. Vikram's body lay on the bed, drenched in a pool of blood. A slight movement near his neck caught her eye. When she saw what it was, she couldn't even scream.

Chhaya looked up at her, still gnawing at Vikram's flesh. Blood dripped from her mouth as she smiled, her teeth chillingly familiar—the same grotesque fangs from Binita's nightmare.

The sight was too much to bear. Even the bravest would have faltered. Binita's vision blurred, and the world around her collapsed into darkness.

When she regained consciousness, disjointed images swam before her eyes. Hands bound. A chair. People weeping.

She recognised the voices of her in-laws. There was shouting, wailing. Some words reached her, others slipped past, muffled in the chaos.

Then a voice rang out—sharp, accusatory.

"Murderer!"

"She's a witch!" another cried—a voice Binita recognised.

"Die, witch!" someone else spat.

Binita squinted, trying to focus. She was in the middle of the courtyard, surrounded by a crowd of about twenty people. Blood stained her sari. Panic gripped her as the reality of Vikram's death sank in.

She wept uncontrollably. The weight of the loss was crushing.

"Look at her! She's laughing!" a voice sneered.

"Shameless!" others chimed in.

"She killed Brinda. And Vikram."

"No!" Binita gasped, trying to protest. "How could you say that?"

But her words drowned in the commotion. She barely had the strength to fight back. Her throat was parched, and every inch of her body ached—her hands, her cheek, her head. A sharp, throbbing pain hinted at a fresh wound.

"Let's burn her!" a young boy suggested.

"She deserves this," another youngster concurred.

"Wait!" Binita wet her lips and tried to form words, her mouth barely moving. "Water...I need... water..."

"Don't give her anything!" her mother-in-law snapped. "She took my son away from me."

"That's not true!" Binita whispered, tears spilling from her eyes.

"I say we burn her!" the same voice insisted.

"Yes! Yes!" the crowd chanted in unison.

Just then, Binita's eyes fell on Chhaya, peeking out from the storeroom. It toddled towards the courtyard, unnoticed by the distracted crowd.

"Wait! You don't understand," Binita could barely get the words out.

"She will hurt you," she tried to warn.

"Die! Die!" the crowd continued.

"Run! Please! Chhaya will eat you," Binita pleaded.

"What is she saying?" someone in the crowd asked.

Suddenly, the air grew still. Chhaya had leapt onto a young boy advancing towards Binita with a burning torch. She latched onto his neck, her small body jerking violently. The force was so great that the boy's entire body moved with her. The scene left everyone aghast.

"What is that!" someone screamed.

The critter lifted her head and hissed at the crowd. Her jagged, needle-like teeth gleamed—a sight that would haunt them if they survived that wretched day.

A man charged forward with a baton, but before he could strike, Chhaya pounced. His screams were cut short as his intestines spilt onto the ground.

Chaos and confusion erupted in the crowd. People ran for their lives. The critter tore through them one by one, ripping limbs, shredding flesh, and dismantling their bodies. Some scrambled to lock themselves inside, while others desperately searched for weapons. But before they could even lift a tool, their hands were mangled beyond use.

Within seconds, the courtyard was bathed in red. When the last body fell silent, Chhaya curled up in Binita's lap, purring as if nothing had happened.

"No… What have you done, Chhaya?" Binita whispered, her voice heavy with horror, fatigue and pain. Chhaya purred contentedly, brushing her head against Binita's lap.

Outside, a lone survivor, dragging a mutilated leg, managed to limp away. He screamed at the top of his lungs, warning the village of the horror he had just witnessed.

"It's the end! It's the end!"

Many Chhayapur villagers laughed from the safety of their homes, amused by the madman's hysteria. A few men gathered around him, both curious and horrified by the sight of blood.

Painful as it was, the man tried to recount what he had seen, gasping for breath as he spoke, only to falter midway. He had spotted an army of disfigured toddlers advancing towards the village. Then, a trilling sound echoed from the rooftop. The moment he looked up, he lost his head—literally.

Chaos spread as people scrambled to bolt their doors, but nothing could shield them from the reckoning of their sins.

Chhayapur's end was near.

# The Lady in Red

When people ask why *The Haunted Castle* (THC) was shut down, only a few know the answer. Speculations abound about the events that led to foreign investors pulling the plug on a multi-billion-dollar deal that was supposed to take the project global. However, there's no denying that THC's downfall was tied to the mysterious disappearance of its billionaire owner, Jared Dale.

A sharp, handsome, and witty man, Jared was in his thirties when he inaugurated *The Haunted Castle*. It marked the beginning of a new economic era. The small town of Morunde had not witnessed anything like it in a lifetime. The news spread like wildfire, and the market boomed. Stocks hit record highs. Everyone was excited about the exhilarating adventure that Jared had laid before them. Tourism flourished, creating countless employment opportunities for the people of Morunde.

Ask any local about it, and they will describe it as the golden age of Morunde. People were happy. Jared's project not only provided them with unparalleled entertainment but also ensured economic stability. The locals saw Jared as their saviour—a God-sent visionary who uplifted a broken and destitute town.

Jared discovered Morunde by accident. No other town in the state celebrated Halloween with such enthusiasm. Morundians were obsessed with horror. Inspired by the horror frenzy in a Morunde pub, Jared, along with his friend Shawn, envisioned the grand plan of creating an entire haunted castle piece by piece.

Shawn was Jared's age. They had been college buddies. He always believed in Jared, even when the world didn't. To him, Jared was a prodigal genius. Though Jared's plans were often over the top, and he always went all in, Shawn stood by him through thick and thin.

*The Haunted Castle* was a meticulously planned venture. Jared envisioned a mammoth project—something the world had never seen before. He took the average haunted house concept, which relied on cheap thrills, and transformed it into something extraordinary. His castle offered an eerie tour with a uniquely terrifying experience. Unlike traditional haunted houses, THC allowed visitors to step into a horror story, making them the protagonists of the narrative. Every month, new stories were written, immersing visitors in an RPG-style horror theme where their choices determined the outcome.

Screams reverberated through the castle corridors. To a passerby, it might seem as though someone was being tortured. The timid stayed away, while adventurers and thrill-seekers never missed a show. They emerged terrified, shaken to the core, while children often ended up wetting their pants.

Jared and his crew loved to experiment. Sometimes, the story was gory, enhanced by realistic props for maximum effect. It was a spectacular cinematic experience within the castle's walls—so authentic that it was difficult to distinguish from reality.

The incredible team at THC meticulously handled every detail of each story. Security cameras were strategically placed throughout the castle to monitor events. Room managers utilized night vision to address any production issues with precision. If a story failed to instil enough fear, it was promptly scrapped. New lines were crafted and implemented on the spot, with improvisation happening in the blink of an eye. The team was extensive, their work demanding, and their hefty salaries justified.

The first week of THC was an enormous success, attracting visitors from around the world eager to experience the hype. Tickets sold like crazy. It was a scream fest. The horror was so intense that it left people with nightmares for days. To maintain the experience, arrangements were made to prevent repeat visits until the story had changed.

With this level of success, some claimed that Jared had managed to create a drug—THC's horror was addictive. It reeled people in effortlessly with its extraordinary atmosphere. Visitors were mesmerised by the castle's ethereal interiors, and the adventure left them talking about it for days. Those who had experienced a story longed to return for more.

The castle seemed to beckon them with its mysteries. Once inside, it was a world of its own. You lived every morsel of fear. You breathed it in. You questioned your sanity, desperate for the nightmare to end. You lost all sense of time. And when you finally emerged, it felt as though you had been trapped for days.

The castle made you a part of it, as if you were an inscription on its walls—forced to witness every horrifying event unfold, powerless to intervene. Inside, you were stripped of control. Every action was futile. It played with human psychology, gnawing at fear until even the boldest felt timid and helpless. Many left with tears in their eyes. Jared had left no stone unturned in crafting a truly terrifying experience, and it showed on the faces of those who survived the ordeal.

At the end of every month, Jared held a conference with his writers to take questions from the press. Reporters from all over the world attended. Every new storyline was kept under wraps, with only the backdrop hinted at to build anticipation days before it was brought to life.

Once, a reporter asked Jared, "Do you believe in ghosts?"

Jared put on his diplomatic hat and replied, "It's not a matter of what I believe. It's a matter of what my audience believes. If they believe in it, my job is to make sure they get a real taste of it."

"How far are you willing to go?" someone in the crowd asked.

"Yes, how real can you make it?" came the follow-up question.

Jared turned to the man who had questioned his limits and replied calmly, "I will make your nightmares come true."

The audience erupted in applause. Jared did not take his eyes off the man until the clapping died down. The truth was, people always got what they signed up for. No one ever complained. Jared became the most successful businessman in no time.

It was during one of these routine post-story interviews that Jared was first asked about the lady in the red dress.

All eyes were on Jared when he turned to face the reporter, "I'm sorry, what?"

"You know, the lady who was seen in the Dark Eyes story—what's that about?"

"What about her?" Jared tried to buy time as he glanced at his crew, who looked equally clueless.

"Is she part of a new storyline? She seemed a little out of place, like a broken strand."

His awkward silence could have sparked murmurs had he not quickly covered it up with, "Oh yeah! You're talking about the Lady in Red. That's something we are experimenting with. We might include it in our next story."

More questions started flying when Jared abruptly stood up and said, "We're going to cut this short today. I have an important call to make. Thanks for coming."

Escaping a sea of a thousand questions, Jared signalled his assistant to arrange an impromptu meeting with his crew. The meeting couldn't wait—Jared had been pacing up and down his office, trying to figure out what the reporter had been talking about.

Once all his crew members had arrived, he nearly shouted, "What the hell was that about?"

Dennis, his lead writer, replied, "We discussed it amongst ourselves…"

"And?" Jared didn't let him finish.

"So far, no one has a clue," Dennis concluded.

"Jim, Peter, Chan—you guys go through the video recordings and check for any anomalies. Roger, Lina, Wendy—you go through the logs. Peter and Jamie…" he paused to take a breath before continuing, "…do a background check on the reporter who asked the question. See how legit he is. Shawn, you're coming with me to review the full story. Let's do a complete walkthrough and leave no stone unturned."

About an hour later, when the whole team assembled again, they shared their results.

"Nothing."

"That son of a bitch was lying to us." Jared looked across the room at Peter and Jamie.

They shrugged. "Looks legit to us."

Jared took a deep breath before concluding, "Alright. We need to be better prepared for future conferences to avoid surprises like this. Hopefully, they'll forget all about it once the next story hits the road."

But it wasn't long before the dreaded question resurfaced at the next post-story conference.

"Why didn't we see the Lady in Red this time?"

"Oh, we're saving her for another story," Jared was quick to reply before moving on to the next question. He was secretly smug that nobody made a fuss this time, and the conference went smoothly. Maybe it had been a technical error after all.

As more stories were released, the crew disregarded the Lady in Red as a minor glitch. Jared was pleased with how things were going. However, his complacency was short-lived.

At the next post-story conference, the topic returned.

"She was terrifying!" a man from the audience exclaimed as soon as a reporter pointed out her presence in the Bahamas story.

Jared looked at his crew again, peeved that the rumoured lady had clawed her way back into their lives. He made a note of everyone who claimed to have seen her. At the end of the conference, he instructed his team to split up for a questionnaire.

"It's part of a research program to make our next story scarier," he reassured anyone who raised an eyebrow.

Thorough research was conducted again, but there was no trace of the Lady in Red in the footage.

The next day, Jared stood outside an inquiry room, watching his subjects through a one-way window they weren't aware existed. One by one, people stepped in to describe the woman who had Jared and his crew on edge.

"In which room did you see her exactly?" Jamie asked the last man on her list. He had a stout build—almost impossible to believe that even someone like him could be horrified by make-believe stories.

"I don't remember where. Aren't you aware of her whereabouts? You're the one who put her in the story," he grunted.

"Sir, this is just a survey. Also, I'm in a different department—I don't know what goes on in a story. These are standard questions prepared by another team. Please answer them so we can all go home quickly," Jamie responded sharply. It was clear that she was fed up with the one-on-one interviews.

Jamie was convinced that there was no foul play and that every attendee was telling the truth. Her patience had been tested incessantly, as she had heard the same versions of the event over and over again from every interviewee.

The man nodded and continued describing the room where he had presumably seen her.

"At first, she was just standing there in one corner. I could barely see the silhouette, but I knew something was there. Her robes were waving in the air. When I got distracted by something else, I noticed she had moved a little closer than before. Then, all of a sudden, she was right underneath the hanging light bulb. I couldn't see her face—it was so dark. But it was horrifying."

Five minutes later, Peter handed Jamie a cup of coffee while the rest of the team was busy preparing a report. Someone suggested calling the local sheriff to report the incident. Jared snapped back, "We have a reputation to maintain. This cannot go out at any cost. We will…"

Jared choked on his words when his eyes fell on a doodle of the Lady in Red. Katie, their sketch artist, had been drawing it during the sessions based on the narratives. The creature that she had drawn was faceless. Her hair might have looked less hideous if Katie hadn't been such a skilled artist. The lady's feet were not visible, as the dress casually obscured the finer details.

Jared wanted to say something, but the unease of looking at the eerie image seemed to have entranced him. Meekly, he muttered, "We've done enough. Let's call it a day!"

Sleep eluded Jared that night. His mind kept elaborating on Katie's drawing, blending it with the vivid descriptions he had heard throughout the day. Every corner of his room felt darker. He switched on every light in the house. Fixing himself a glass of wine, he paused on his way back to stand in front of a mirror, trying to calm himself down.

*"It's nothing. You're thinking too much, Jared!"*

The next sip made him realise—he hadn't been drinking wine. Blood dripped from the corners of his mouth. His eyes widened in horror as he looked at his reflection. Shocked, he dropped the glass. It shattered, spilling good wine.

*"What is wrong with me?"*

The next day, he couldn't concentrate on the new story idea his writers were pitching. His eyes kept drifting towards Katie. She was wearing a blood-red sweater.

"Why are you wearing red today?"

Katie gave him a puzzled look. The rest of the staff exchanged glances, unable to understand where the question was coming from.

"Are you trying to make a point?" Jared pressed, his voice sharper now.

"Jared, are you okay?" Jamie asked, reaching out to touch his hand, trying to break the awkward tension.

Jared looked at Jamie and nodded. The meeting continued, but he was no longer paying attention. His eyes scanned the room, only to notice several other staff members wearing red.

"Nobody will wear red going forward," Jared announced before pretending to focus on the meeting. Puzzled glances were exchanged, but nobody said a word.

The next day, as Jared walked with Shawn, discussing plans, he noticed someone standing in the castle hallway. Her back was turned, so he couldn't see her face. But what instantly enraged him was the colour of her dress—red. Cutting Shawn off mid-sentence, Jared stormed towards the girl in fury.

"Did I not tell you not to wear red?" He demanded, grabbing her hand to turn her around. To his horror, she didn't move. Instead, her face emerged from the back of her head, her hair parting to either side. Blood seeped from her skin as she crooned, "But all I have is red."

Frozen in terror, Jared felt his grip loosen as her blood-slicked hand slipped from his grasp, lifeless. Her robe billowed as she drifted into the darkness.

Jared collapsed to the ground, gasping. "Did you see that? Tell me you saw that!" he pleaded.

Shawn took a deep breath and nodded. "I saw it."

For the rest of the day, Jared couldn't stop talking about the Lady in Red. To many, it seemed like an obsession.

"What's gotten into him?" people whispered.

"I think he's losing it," someone murmured.

But no one dared to say it aloud.

That evening, while they were having snacks, Shawn approached Jared with a coffee mug in his hand. Jared looked tense, glancing over his shoulder.

"Listen, Jared, the team is a little worried," Shawn mentioned.

"Worried? About what?" Jared asked, not meeting his gaze.

"This Lady in Red obsession is getting a little out of hand."

"Obsession? Are you out of your mind? I saw her, Shawn! I saw her, and you saw her too—didn't you?" Jared's voice wavered.

Shawn took a slow sip from his mug before replying, "I didn't see anything."

Jared froze. "What? But you said..." Realisation struck him like a blow. "Why did you lie to me?"

"I just didn't want you to feel alone," Shawn admitted.

"Alone? Am I alone in this? You heard everyone's stories!" Jared was indignant.

"Yes, and I still think there's a rational explanation for all of this," Shawn said, placing a reassuring hand on Jared's shoulder. "Whatever it is, we'll figure it out."

Jared exhaled sharply. "Am I losing my mind, Shawn?"

"No. You're not," Shawn said firmly. "But I'll be honest with you. At one point, I was in a similar situation."

Jared's brow furrowed.

"Yes, I saw things too. Then I met someone who explained how, when you constantly work on a project like this, it can take a toll on you," Shawn continued.

Jared still looked disoriented.

"Don't let this consume you, Jared. Look around." Shawn gestured towards the room with his mug.

"We live and breathe horror. Sometimes, it gets to us, and it is completely fine. You know why, Jared? Because we're human."

Shawn rummaged through his pocket and pulled out a card. "Here. This is the psychiatrist I saw. He's in LA—hands down the best shrink you'll ever meet."

Jared took the card and looked at Shawn. "Do you think I'm crazy?"

"It is not about you. It's about everything we've built here. Do you really want to throw it all away?" Shawn's voice was solemn.

There was a rare gravity in his tone that made Jared look at the staff in the room. Everyone seemed to be having a good time.

"No. Definitely not. This is my life," he said, determination creeping back into his voice.

"Then trust me. We've got this," Shawn said, squeezing Jared's shoulder.

Jared forced a smile.

On the flight to LA, Jared couldn't stop replaying the past few sleepless nights. The image of the Lady in Red haunted him. Her touch had felt so real.

How could he have possibly imagined her?

He took out the card that Shawn had given him. It read 'Greg Davies.' He flipped it over to check the address, then tilted his head back, hoping to catch a few winks, but he kept looking out the window. The clouds looked comfortable, fluffy and still. They made him miss his exquisite bed, his mattress, comforter, and countless fluffy pillows. He could almost taste a good night's sleep.

When the next announcement came, his eyes flickered open almost uncontrollably. But he realised that he could not move. His line of sight showed the vantage outside, where the clouds appeared motionless. The sun had dispersed its rays, emanating an orangish hue.

"*How long has it been?*" he thought.

There was sudden movement on the horizon, where the clouds merged with the sky. Something black emerged from the far end. It looked like hair. It began sifting through the clouds as they parted, allowing it to wade through. The hair dipped again, disappearing beneath the clouds, only to return—this time, a tad closer. It seemed as if someone was wading through them.

He heard someone shout in the background, "Mayday! Mayday!"

There was chaos and confusion. He could hear the passengers screaming. Someone pointed and gasped, "What is that?"

The sky slowly began changing colour. The figure dipped again, vanishing, then reemerging—this time, its features more distinct. Jared felt like a sitting duck, unable to move, watching the horror unfold. He tried to shift his legs, but they wouldn't budge. The cloud-swimmer inched closer to the plane, lifting itself higher, making its face crystal clear. Jared recognised it almost instantly. How could he forget those eyes?

Sweat trickled down his forehead. The Lady in Red took another dive, disappearing completely— as if she had merged with the clouds. Silence permeated the cabin. The clouds gradually took on the colour of her robes, swirling in eerie, hypnotic movements, floating just as they had during the incident in the hallway. Jared had been so focused on the diving figure that he had failed to notice the subtle atmospheric shift that had happened within seconds. The sun was now a red blob. Jared could feel the searing rays sink their teeth into his skin.

Then suddenly, she emerged again—larger this time. The Lady in Red opened her mouth wide, breaking the wings of the plane in the process, lunging forward to devour everything in sight. Jared stared into her blood-red eyes, paralyzed with fear, as she sank her teeth into the tiny window through which he was watching.

Suddenly, he jolted awake.

Beside him, children were playing games on their mobile phones. A flight attendant was chatting with an elderly couple. A pair laughed in the background.

Jared looked out the window. Everything was blue. The clouds were intact. Soon, they would be preparing to land.

Greg was a man in his fifties. A pair of spectacles hung precariously at the edge of his long nose. He looked up from his notes at his client.

"And this..." Greg hesitated, seemingly forgetting the name.

"...Lady in Red," Jared filled in the blank.

"Yes. How long have you been seeing her?" asked Greg.

"It's been a month now," replied Jared without thinking too hard.

"Tell me the first time you saw her," Greg prompted.

Greg had asked Jared to return to a memory he dreaded—a dark place he wasn't ready to revisit. But the insistence was for the sake of treatment.

Jared took a deep breath and then tried to recollect the hallway incident before continuing, "I was in the hallway with Shawn. We were discussing a new story idea we were working on when I saw a girl standing at one end of the hallway. I was distracted by her presence because I had specifically asked my staff not to wear red."

"And why is that, Jared?" Greg interposed.

"Because—well, it sounds stupid—but red reminded me of a dream I had the other night, or maybe a hallucination..." Jared continued.

"Hallucinations?" Greg looked up from his notes.

"Yes…it was…" As Jared tried to reply, he was distracted by a girl who had just emerged from a room and sat next to Greg on the sofa.

Jared looked questioningly at Greg, as if seeking an introduction.

"Please continue," Greg replied calmly.

"It was nothing," Jared sighed, putting both his hands on his head, trying to wave the incident off.

"Jared, I need to hear the whole account if you want my help," Greg pressed.

Jared did not respond. He stared at the girl sitting next to the shrink. Her arms were folded as if she were upset about something. Her eyes were fixated on the floor.

"Ok, so did you approach the girl in the hallway?" Greg asked.

"Yes, I did," Jared replied, brought back to the story.

"What did she say?" Greg asked.

"I don't remember… Wait, I think she said…" Jared struggled to recall.

"All I have is red." The girl sitting on the sofa completed his sentence.

She had looked up for the first time. Now, she was staring directly at Jared.

Jared tried to scream, but his voice eluded him. He kept looking at her, dumbstruck. It was her—

the Lady in Red—sitting right next to Greg, who seemingly had no clue of her presence.

For the first time, Jared noticed that she was wearing red. The lady suddenly got up and began retching. A stream of blood vented from her mouth, splattering onto Jared's face.

Jared's eyes shut, his body constricting in a defensive pose.

"What is it, Jared? Are you okay?"

When he opened his eyes, he saw a confused Greg, now keenly aware of Jared's uncalled-for behaviour.

"Where did she go?" asked Jared.

"Where did who go?" Greg looked bewildered.

"The girl?" Jared was adamant.

"What girl, Jared?" Greg asked, disturbed.

"The girl... the Lady in Red," Jared managed to answer meekly.

"Jared, it has been just you and me in this room the whole time," replied Greg.

"What? You didn't see her? She was right there, sitting next to you!" Jared pointed at the sofa.

He sprang up and frantically searched the room for the Lady in Red.

"She came from inside," Jared muttered as he searched the adjoining rooms.

"Jared! Jared!" Greg tried to call after him.

"I swear she was here, Greg," Jared replied helplessly as he returned.

"Okay, calm down," replied Greg. "I believe you. What else do you see?"

Jared could not believe it. He was pulling at his hair now.

"Jared, wait," Greg tried to stop him. But it was too late—Jared had already stormed out of Greg's office.

"Wait, where are you going? Jared, we're not done!" Greg kept calling after him, but to no avail.

Outside, the city was alive with a swarm of people, the hustle and bustle accounting for its restless energy. Engines purred, shoes struck the pavement, voices clashed in heated exchanges, whistles shrieked, phones rang, and sirens wailed in the distance. But for poor Jared, it was blood everywhere. Every shade of red stood out, searing his vision, demanding his attention.

To a passerby, Jared looked like a madman, his eyes darting in every direction at once. He kept walking, hoping—praying—not to run into the Lady in Red again. But it was a futile wish.

Soon enough, silence pervaded. The din of the city died down. Every person on the street had stopped to look at him. Then, on every face Jared saw, he saw her—the Lady in Red—staring at him with those judgmental eyes.

Jared clutched his head and sank to the ground.

*"I'm losing my mind."*

Tears welled in his eyes. Between his trembling fingers, he peeked at the crowd moving towards him, closing in like a tightening noose. He was paralyzed by fear—trapped in a nightmare while fully awake.

Then, his eyes fell on a crowbar resting near a doorway, just inches away.

*"I can't go on like this. It has to stop. I have to do something."*

Desperation propelled him forward. He scrambled towards the crowbar, seized it, and swung wildly. But within seconds, reality snapped back into place. The city noise returned. The onlookers were ⊠ck to normal—some watching in horror, others calling him crazy. A few muttered complaints about the danger he posed.

The cacophony of life had resumed.

That night, as Jared stepped out of his car in Morunde, the sky erupted in thunder. The sudden shift in weather was already making headlines. "So, *it's going to rain after all*," he thought, making his way inside his mansion.

"Sir, there's a power outage," said the butler, holding a candle in his hand. "I called the office to check—they said it's due to the storm."

"Just what I needed to hear," Jared scoffed, heading to his room.

Candlelight flickered through the dim halls, casting restless shadows. Jared decided to shower first. When he stepped out, his drink had already been fixed alongside his dinner. It had been a crazy day, after all.

In the vast, dimly lit dining hall, he sat at one end, eating in silence. Then a strange sound interrupted him—the unmistakable noise of chewing.

He stopped.

The sound stopped.

He resumed eating.

The sound followed.

Jared's gaze drifted to the other end of the long table. In the flickering candlelight, he noticed that a plate had been set there.

He held his breath as he heard the distinct clink of a fork against the plate.

A single pea tumbled off, rolling towards him.

"Max! Max!" he called out to his butler—then froze.

The pea was gradually changing, its form shifting, distorting.

It was no longer a pea.

It was an eyeball.

From the darkness ahead, what he had mistaken for a fork was, in fact, a grotesque set of fingernails.

They plunged towards him—fast, deliberate. Jared was paralyzed, unable to move.

But instead of clawing him, one of the nails speared the fleshy eyeball, skewering it in one swift motion before vanishing into oblivion.

"What is it, Master?" Max appeared out of nowhere and stood next to Jared.

"Thank God you're here! Max! Who's there?" Jared could barely point.

"Who's where, sir?" Max replied.

"There! There! Look there..." Jared pointed frantically towards the other end of the table.

"I can't see properly, let me just..." Max rubbed his eye.

For the first time, Jared looked at Max's face—and froze. Max had only one eye. He had been rubbing the empty socket where the other should have been. Then, out of nowhere, he collapsed in front of Jared, his head striking the table with a sickening thud. His remaining eye popped out, rolling across the table until it came to a stop at the far end.

Jared watched in utter shock as the hand returned—its fingernail glinting in the candlelight—piercing the fallen eye like a fork before vanishing once more into the darkness. The wet, guttural chewing that followed sent a shiver down Jared's spine.

"That's it!" Jared lunged towards his room, death burning in his eyes. He reached beneath his pillow, his fingers closing around the cold metal of his gun.

Holding a candle in his other hand, he scoured the dark.

"Where are you? What do you want from me?" he shouted like a madman.

Just then, the candle flickered—and died.

The darkness swallowed him whole.

Something brushed against his arm.

The night erupted with gunfire.

A few minutes later, the screech of tyres pierced the silence as a car sped towards the castle.

Shawn's slumber was shattered by the shrill ringing of his landline. He groggily checked the time.

1:00 AM.

He immediately recognised the voice of a breathless Simon, the man in charge of castle security.

"Sir, sir…sorry to call you so late," Simon panted.

"Calm down, Simon. What happened?" Shawn asked, rubbing the sleep from his eyes.

"Sir, Jared Dale drove through the gates—he had a gun in his hand," Simon gasped.

"What?" Shawn couldn't believe it.

"Yes, sir, he didn't look himself," Simon revealed.

"Call the police. I'll be there in ten minutes." Shawn jumped out of bed and grabbed his keys.

When Jared stepped out of the car, a raindrop fell onto his hand. He looked at it. The water droplet was red. Suddenly, the skies bled.

He ran for cover inside the nearest tower. Reaching the stairwell, he hurried towards the hallway, where he had last seen the Lady in Red. He moved cautiously in the darkness, each step measured. He reached for the main switch, but the storm had already wiped out the town's power.

Every sound made him flinch, terror creeping in with every passing second. When he heard a noise from one of the rooms, he barged in without a second thought. It was one of the haunted rooms his team had created. His macabre designs were lined up like dolls in a twisted playhouse.

He knew each creation by heart, so he moved past them, following the noise into the next room. When the door opened to the third room, every mechanical element whirred to life. He shook off the unsettling thought of the empty control room and focused on spotting anything that deviated from the script he had memorized.

One by one, as he passed through the rooms, Jared relived the stories he had once conceived. He knew that the little girl by the window would try to scare him. That in the next room, a mechanical arm would clutch at his leg. Every detail was familiar as he effortlessly flipped through the pages he had overseen with his team. Yet, with each passing moment, the possibility of an unforeseen surprise loomed over him—the only thing that bothered him in his own playground.

He was about to grow restless when he spotted a red door.

*"This wasn't part of the story,"* he thought.

Treading carefully, he approached it. Before turning the knob, he cast a glance back at his creation, as if standing at the threshold between life and death. Anything could happen in the next few minutes. A sudden thought struck him—there was no one to say goodbye to.

Taking a deep breath, he opened the door. A red light flooded the room. He stepped inside and found himself standing at the centre of an empty space, as a single spotlight beamed down from above. He looked up, searching for the source—then, he fell.

Jared plunged into nothingness. He flailed, grasping at the empty air, desperate to hold onto something— anything. But there was nothing.

It was the day of reckoning. He was not of pure heart. As he fell, he relived every wicked deed he had ever committed. His sins flashed before him, one by one. The gun he had used to silence voices. The empire he had built on the graves of the fallen. The people he had destroyed, all in the name of business. His arrogance, his cruelty.

A mirror of conscience appeared before him. In the reflection, he recoiled at the face he saw—the face of a murderer, a cheat, a trickster.

Then, his feet touched the ground. He collapsed to his knees, breathless. It felt as if he had been falling for an eternity. The red light was gone. The room was empty.

Jared was consumed by an overwhelming sense of despondency. He knew he didn't deserve to live. His grip tightened around the gun in his hand. Raising to his mouth, he prepared to pull the trigger.

Then, from the darkness, the wavy robes emerged—the same ones from their first encounter. A whisper slithered from the void.

*"That would be an easy escape."*

Shawn was the second to reach the castle, with Simon following close behind, lantern in hand. They rushed towards the keep, where the castle's office was. Finding it empty, they split up to search for Jared.

Then came the gunshot.

Shawn bolted towards the noise, rushing through the rooms until he reached the last one. He pushed open the door—and stopped.

Jared stood in the center, his back to him. A red spotlight drenched him in an otherworldly glow. He seemed to be looking upward.

"Jared!" Shawn called.

He barely took a step when something emerged from Jared's front. Strands of black hair. A pair of gleaming eyes. The thing stared at Shawn as its mouth stretched wide, sinking its teeth into Jared's throat. The crimson robe of the Lady in Red coiled around him.

Shawn's hand shot towards the emergency switch on the wall. He flipped it.

The room blazed with light, illuminating a space that had long felt dead. Shawn's breath came in short gasps as he scanned the room.

Jared and the Lady in Red were gone.

He stepped forward. The room was just another exhibit—haunted artifacts from THC lined the walls like eerie souvenirs. There were paintings, pictures, models, games, and statuettes of the very horror they had once created.

Ten minutes later, the local sheriff arrived, Simon close behind. The officer approached Shawn, who was still reeling from what he had witnessed.

"Where is Jared?"

Shawn swallowed hard. "He... he disappeared."

The news of Jared's mysterious disappearance spread like wildfire. THC was shut down overnight. Every investor backed out.

Shawn returned to the castle often, revisiting the last room where Jared had vanished. But no matter how many times he tried, he couldn't make sense of what had happened. The police dismissed his account as too absurd to be true.

One month later, upon hearing that the castle was to be sealed permanently, Shawn visited one last time. To him, it felt like a final tribute to Jared before moving on. In the final room, his eyes fell on a chessboard in the corner. A single black pawn lay toppled over. He picked it up and set it upright.

Before leaving, he took one last look at the world he was leaving behind—a life he would miss, a life he would likely never return to.

In the silence of that room, Shawn couldn't hear the desperate cries of the man trapped within.

Jared had been shouting all this time from the chessboard, his voice lost to the void.

"Shawn! Shawn! Don't leave! I'm here. I'm stuck here! Come back! Come back! Shawn!"

As Shawn stepped out, Jared let out one final, anguished scream, "Shawn! No! Don't leave me here!" His voice broke into helpless sobs.

It was a life that was no longer a life. A death that was not quite a death. Jared had woven himself into his own creation, becoming nothing more than a piece in his own twisted story.

The king had become a pawn.

With THC shut down, Katie, the sketch artist, had been stuck in her room for a while. She had created countless paintings, hoping to sell them on a platform she planned to launch. After all, she had plenty of contacts and people willing to help. She often reassured herself that she would bounce back in no time. Yet, for some reason, she couldn't find the inspiration to leave town. She had a history there—how could she just walk away?

One day, inspiration struck, and she spent hours painting. By the time she finished, it was almost evening. She admired her creation for a while, murmuring to herself, *"Katie, you outdid yourself!"*

When her phone buzzed, she stepped out, leaving the exquisite painting of The Lady in Red behind on the easel. Shawn had come to bid her farewell—he was leaving town.

After Katie returned to her room, her heart felt heavy. Shawn's departure made one thing painfully clear—THC was gone for good. The dream of rejoining it was shattered. Something good had ended. The chapter of her life was over. She was so lost in thought that she failed to notice the painting she had admired just hours ago—the Lady in Red, which she always painted without eyes, now had eyes.

Late that night, after finishing her chores, Katie returned to bed. She was about to switch off the light when something caught her eye. The painting looked eerily real, as if the Lady in Red was standing right beside her bed. A chill ran down Katie's spine. She turned the light back on, her breath hitching at the sight of two pairs of eyes staring into nothingness.

She was still trying to process how the eyes had appeared when—suddenly—they shifted and locked onto her.

For a second, Katie's heart stopped. Before she could move, the Lady in Red emerged from the canvas, the pages of the painting clinging to her like tattered clothes, blood oozing from every tear. She lunged onto the bed, her red robes swallowing them both as she dragged Katie into an unknown world.

Days later, the police investigated yet another recondite disappearance—this time from a locked room. An officer lingered near the easel, studying the lifelike painting by the bed.

He murmured, "Why did Katie paint herself?"

# UNDER THE BANYAN TREE

Near a small school in the village of Kapagarh stood a massive banyan tree resting on a cemented base, often used by villagers as a place to sit and relax. Next to the tree, several workshops had been set up by local labourers, though none were in operation. People claimed that some of the workers had died there, while the rest had left for the city in search of better opportunities. However, their dilapidated shops remained standing, untouched.

One evening, a group of children was playing dodgeball in the school playground. Their ball was made by tying multiple socks into knots. A hit was considered good if it landed squarely on the back of a running child. Every successful strike was followed by fits of laughter. The game was an absolute riot, especially when someone tripped over their shoelaces and tumbled into a pile of mud. Hilarious!

As the sun neared the horizon, the chirping of retreating birds was gradually lost among the frantic tweets of the children. In the back of their minds, many knew it was time to head home, but few were willing to say it out loud, not wanting to miss out on the fun. What felt like mere moments stretched into minutes until Kavit, a 15-year-old boy and the strongest among them, threw the ball with such force that it soared past the banyan tree.

Beneath the gnarled branches of the lone tree, three workers huddled together, their faces hidden in shadow. They appeared to be eating something. Two children ran towards them, hoping to get one of the men's attention.

The first child blurted out, "Uncle! Throw the ball this way."

The workers appeared unperturbed by the call, seemingly engrossed in their meal.

"Hey! You! I'm talking to you! Are you deaf?" the child exclaimed, frustration creeping into his voice.

Soon, the rest of the children came in, chanting, "Uncle! Ball! Ball! Please throw our ball back."

Kavit, impatient and bold, shouted bluntly, "Oh! Deaf people!"

Miffed by the lack of response, he picked up a stone and hurled it at them. That was when the dark figures finally turned.

As they moved, the children caught a glimpse of something white in their mouths, covered in blood. Feathers were strewn across the platform. The figures were feasting on a white heron. The stone attack had enraged them. Without warning, all three shadowy forms pranced towards the children.

They had no legs, no defined shape. Their bodies hovered above the ground as they glided forward. They moved in eerie, unnatural motions, closing the distance with terrifying speed.

A hissing sound rose from behind as the children ran for their lives.

"Ghost! Ghost!" they shrieked, their voices piercing the evening air as they scattered in every direction, bolting towards home.

Upon returning home in one piece, the children made sure that no one had been left behind in the commotion. That evening's events were recounted again and again to their parents. While some were scolded, others were forbidden from playing in the dark. It was unanimously agreed that no one would venture near the banyan tree.

That night, two children came down with a fever, but they recovered within a day or two.

Kavit lived in a house that overlooked the banyan tree. He had often heard a hissing noise coming from that direction but had always dismissed it as birds or animals fighting over food. He had never given it much thought until that night.

Even now, when Kavit struggles to sleep, he finds himself attributing the night's noises to surreal happenings around the tree. His mind replays the events of that night, relentlessly trying to put a face to those dark figures.

An undeniable and unsettling anomaly has taken root in our familiar world—and it continues to linger around the banyan tree.

# EIGHT

"How far is it?" Jane Brown asked, her patience wearing thin. The 24-year-old teacher from Pueblo had envisioned a fun getaway, but so far, the trip had been anything but. Behind the wheel was Harry Brown, her 30-year-old husband, an accountant from Reuben. Eager for a break from their demanding lives, they had planned this trip as an escape. However, due to heavy rainfall, they were running behind.

The couple had first met at a gala event in Pueblo, a chance encounter sparked by Jane's headstrong friend, who had dragged her there against her will. Meanwhile, Harry, who knew the basics of the ukulele, had been urged to perform as a backup for a singer who had suddenly lost his voice. Though his performance received a lukewarm response from the audience, he managed to win the heart of one. Jane fell for him hard. And while Harry strummed, he couldn't take his eyes off her, though it wasn't until later that they officially met, introduced by Jane's friend, who happened to know Harry.

Stars aligned in their favour, with one good thing leading to another, culminating in their marriage two years later. Harry relocated to Pueblo to be with Jane and landed a job in his field. However, the workload was intense, often keeping him at the office late into the night.

One evening, the couple had a heated argument about how little time they spent together. By nightfall, they had decided to spend the weekend at *Adventure-X*, a camping resort near Cuchara, about an hour's drive away.

*Adventure-X* had opened a few years ago and quickly gained popularity for its variety of activities, including archery, trekking, shooting, cycling, zip-lining and bungee jumping. The artificial campsite, known for its tent accommodations, spanned a vast area and could host over fifty families. However, being in the mountains, the roads were poorly maintained, one of the reasons Harry was driving so cautiously.

Jane eyed her husband, expecting a response.

"Almost there," Harry reassured her, his voice calm. He wasn't a reckless driver and preferred to stay vigilant for any surprises.

Outside, the windshield wipers played a symphony while the downpour beat like drums. From time to time, the orchestra grew brutal, shrouding their destination in mist. Yet, they pressed on, piercing through the woods and crawling over the unreliable stretch ahead.

As darkness crept in, Jane grew more restless. "Didn't the GPS say eight kilometres an hour ago? It's still showing eight. I think it's broken," she muttered.

Harry remained silent, though the same thought had been nagging him.

"I don't like this place. It gives me the chills. Anything could happen here, and no one would ever know. I just hope we don't have to drive back in the dark," Jane remarked, pulling her blanket tighter around her.

"Do you want me to turn off the AC?" asked Harry, dodging her discomfort.

"No, it's better this way," she replied with a grin.

As they drove on, a familiar sign emerged from the rain-drenched road—Adventure-X.

"About time," Harry said, pointing at it, relieved to finally see proof of their destination.

"Yay!" Jane deadpanned.

As they made their way in, Harry realised the place wasn't nearly as lively as he remembered. Perhaps it was the off-season, or maybe the initial hype had faded, but Adventure-X now projected a dismal, almost abandoned image.

*"Was coming in the rain a good decision?"* Harry wondered as he scanned the area for a supply shop.

There were no cigarettes or drinks available either. Then there were the rumours, which he had dismissed. Still, he liked the solitude. A break from the city was exactly what he had been craving.

Two years ago, Harry had visited *Adventure-X* with some colleagues and remembered enjoying the sheer tranquility of the place. While others rushed off for adventure sports, he had been content sitting outside his tent, sipping coffee and reading a book. The mountains loomed in the background, and birds peered at him from the bushes. He remembered the carefree warmth of that moment—it had been the very definition of perfection.

Today, it was different. The atmosphere had changed. The weather was ominous. It felt as though he had stepped into a completely different world. Through the heavy downpour, he turned around to look at the mountains, hoping to catch a glimpse of their grandeur—but all he could make out were murky silhouettes.

By the time they reached the reception area, both Harry and Jane were drenched from their dash through the rain from the parking lot. Inside, Harry greeted the receptionist, a short, stout man in his thirties, who barely looked up from his phone, engrossed in a mobile game.

Harry inquired about the availability of tents and other provisions while Jane looked around. The sullen, dome-shaped tents appeared helpless in the rain. The corridors were lit, but some bulbs flickered. She shuddered at the thought of a power cut.

Harry learned that the management planned to light a bonfire soon under a shed, after which dinner would be served in a common dining area.

The receptionist added, "Since it's raining heavily outside, we've set up some tents indoors."

"Defeats the whole purpose of camping, doesn't it?" Harry was furious.

"We had no choice. Believe me, sir, you'll get the same experience," the receptionist tried to reason.

Harry looked at Jane, who was freezing. Her demeanour practically screamed for warm clothes. Harry shot a look at the stickler before pulling out his wallet to make the initial payment. With sarcasm, he said, "You think?"

A few moments later, an attendant led them to their room. They had barely walked a few steps before reaching a unit that opened into several rooms. These rooms shared a common washing area accessible to all residents. Just outside, a small lobby held a table and chair, likely for the unit's attendant. Similar units were scattered across a large garden in the centre.

Upon unlocking their room, Jane and Harry found two tents set up in the middle. Essentials were neatly laid out on the table.

"So they *are* providing you with the experience of camping. Perfect!" Jane remarked slyly as Harry shut the door behind them. They changed into comfortable clothes before heading out for the bonfire.

To reach the bonfire area, they had to dash through an uncovered passage. Not every path had a roof overhead. The fireplace was inside a closed shed, surrounded by benches. The same attendant was busy tending to the fire, tossing in sticks and other flammable materials. Harry and Jane took their seats, rubbing their hands for warmth.

As the bonfire blazed, another family arrived, emerging from a different unit at the far end of the site.

"Should have come during winter," the head of the family grumbled as he took a seat across from Harry and Jane. His wife and teenage son sat beside him. They were whispering to each other, seemingly uninterested in the conversation. All three of them were drenched.

"I am sorry?" Harry assumed the announcement was meant for him.

"This place used to be fun," the man continued. "I remember when we had our tents outside. Nights were never this gloomy."

Harry nodded. "That's exactly what I've been telling Jane. She doesn't seem too impressed so far."

Jane quickly interjected to be polite. "No! No! It's great. It's just the weather playing spoilsport, that's all."

"Yes, the rain has taken away the fun. We should have planned this trip better," the man sighed.

"You got that right," Harry agreed.

The man introduced himself as Dr. Isaac Jenkins, a physicist still in practice. His wife, Melanie, was a teacher, and their son, Jimbo, was still in school. After exchanging pleasantries, they realised they were the only two families visiting that day.

As the fire crackled, conversation drifted into quiet family murmurs.

"Do you know any horror stories?" Jane suddenly asked, breaking the monotony. Huddled around the bonfire, the setup practically begged for a ghost story.

Harry sighed. "Here we go again," he muttered under his breath.

Isaac glanced around, then at his family, before adjusting in his seat. "I could tell you one about this place."

Jane's eyes widened. Harry wondered if Isaac was about to confirm the rumours he had heard about Adventure-X.

"You want to know why people stopped coming here?" Isaac leaned in.

Melanie rolled her eyes. "Oh, come on! You don't believe that nonsense, do you?"

Isaac shrugged, nodding towards Jane. "I am just saying. The girl wants a story."

Jane's heart skipped a beat. "What happened? Please tell me."

Isaac's expression became grave. "Mass murder. Last year. Eight people were killed by a psychopath. He dragged them into the woods one by one, killing them in different ways. It was all over the local news. But the tourism department bribed the authorities to keep it quiet."

He turned to Harry and pointed. "You know how it is around here. Tourism is big money."

Jane clamped her hands over her mouth. "Eight murders?" she mumbled in disbelief. Harry had heard a thing or two about the rumours, but not the specifics.

"They finally got him," Isaac said, staring broodingly into the fire. "It's weird how people get unhinged— the damage they bring in the wake of their insanity. You can't escape from that. All you can do is hope… Hope that you don't end up stranded in the wrong place at the wrong time."

Harry scoffed, wrapping an arm around Jane. "That wasn't bad, was it, dear?"

Isaac moved closer to the fire, its reflection flickering in his eyes. "Now, here comes the big one. Since then, people have claimed to witness ghosts every night— the ghosts of those who were brutally murdered that night. They wander these ridges and hills, seeking solace in this godforsaken place." He looked around before lowering his voice. "Pay close attention, and you might be lucky enough to see one yourself… or should I say unlucky?"

Jane felt a lump in her throat. Isaac's intensity unsettled her. Just then, the dinner bell rang, its clanking sound making everyone jolt. Isaac and his family took their leave while Harry turned to Jane.

"You okay?" he asked nervously.

Jane shot him a glare. "I can't believe you brought us here. Of all the places in the world, you found this shithole? It has a history—for crying out loud."

Harry shrugged, "Oh, come on, Jane. Every place in the world has a history. Aren't they just pages we paint over? Our home was probably a graveyard once. A whole civilization is buried beneath us. No matter where, we're always trampling over the dead. What about dinosaurs? Aren't they all ghosts too?"

Jane was livid. "Oh, please! Spare me the philosophical bullshit. Eight people died here, and it hasn't even been a year."

They stood and walked to the common dining area, where Isaac and his family were already eating chicken.

"Oh, good." Harry teased Jane, pointing at their meal, "We have *you* for dinner."

Jane frowned as she moved towards the plates. Harry ate heartily, having skipped food the entire trip. Exhausted, he wanted to retire early for a promising day of trekking the next day. Jane, however, gave him the silent treatment throughout the meal. Once they were finished, they bid the Jenkins family goodnight and returned to their room.

Still upset, Jane chose to sleep in the second tent, even though one was large enough for both of them. Although the door was shut, she left a dim light on. Her mind kept drifting back to Isaac's story while Harry snored unfazed in his tent.

Jane couldn't sleep—not just because of Jenkins' tale, but because the wooden floorboards occasionally creaked. The thudding sounds suggested someone was moving through the common hall. She assumed it was the receptionist or the attendant.

"Probably using the bathroom," she reassured herself, trying to shake off her anxiety.

But the noise never ceased. Jane remained alert despite her best efforts to ignore it. The tight space of the tent made her uncomfortable, and the room felt unbearably warm despite the fans being on.

She dreaded the moment she'd have to go to the bathroom—an inevitability she fought against. She tried to hold it for as long as she could, but eventually, she had no choice. Reluctantly, she emerged from her tent, unzipped the other one where Harry lay fast asleep, and tugged at him.

"Harry! Wake up. I need to go to the loo," she whispered.

The snoring stopped, but he didn't stir. She tugged at him again.

"Harry! Harry!"

Finally, he groaned, half-asleep. "What? That was such a good dream."

Jane pointed at her pinky. Harry sluggishly rolled over, rubbing his eyes as he struggled to get out of his tent. Still drowsy, he shuffled towards the door to unlock it.

The persistent thumping and creaking of the loose floorboards continued in the background. Jane hoped to see someone outside. But as soon as the door opened, the noise simply died.

Utter darkness loomed beyond their open door. The faint glow from their room barely reached the hall. A man sat in a chair, his back to them, motionless. He seemed to be asleep.

"Must be the attendant," Jane thought as she turned to face Harry.

"I'll be standing right here at the door," Harry reassured her. Too stressed to argue, Jane made her way to the toilet.

When she returned, she found Harry still at the door, struggling to keep his eyes open. She pushed him inside and turned around to close the door. Her eyes caught the chair. It was empty.

"Where did he go?" Jane whispered.

"Who?" Harry asked, groggy.

Jane was certain she had seen a man. "The man— the one who was sitting in that chair."

Harry yawned and dismissed her concern. "I didn't see anybody."

Jane was confused, but it made her even more uptight. Tension mounting, she crawled into Harry's tent, forcing her way in next to him as he grunted in protest.

Not long after, the noise returned. The floor groaned under invisible weight. Loud thumps echoed—a rhythm of someone running or stumbling; it was hard to tell.

"Do you hear that?" Jane whispered urgently.

Harry, too sleepy to care, muttered, "Sleep, detective. Sleep. We have to wake up early for trekking."

"How could you not care?" Jane whispered, lying on her back, eyes fixed on the tent flap.

She doubted anyone could sleep after what she had witnessed.

The floorboards creaked and thumped. The noise persisted. She glanced at Harry. He was already snoring.

"Why can't I be as carefree as him?" she wondered, deciding to deliberately close her eyes for a minute.

"Maybe it's all in my head." She forced herself to relax before succumbing to slumber.

Her eyes fluttered open involuntarily, stirred by the mingling sounds of Harry's snoring and the relentless thumping. The noises began to blend—a monotonous rhythm lulling her into uneasy slumber.

Then, a third sound. A whisper. A breath. A dissonant note in her dreamy world. Her eyes opened slowly to its rhythmic note, adjusting to the dim light.

A silhouette stood at the tent flap. Like a slow-moving tide, her mind processed the figure. The shape sharpened. The man peering at them materialised.

Jane screamed, jolting Harry awake.

"What? What happened?" he asked, his voice thick with confusion.

Jane could barely speak. "A man—he was standing right there!" She pointed towards the tent flap, her hand shaking.

Harry crawled out of the tent, rubbing his face. "What? What man? We're in a closed room. There's nobody here." He flicked on all the lights, illuminating the space.

Wide-eyed and trembling, Jane stepped out of the tent and stood behind Harry, scanning every corner of the room.

"I swear I saw someone. He was right there!" she sobbed, pointing again.

Harry exhaled, frustration creeping in. "But there's no one here. See?" he smacked the side of the tent, the fabric rippling with the impact.

"Why would I make this up?" Jane pleaded.

Harry ignored the question. "How many times have I told you not to watch or listen to horror stories at night?"

"But I saw him," Jane insisted.

"You never listen… " Harry started, but Jane cut him off.

"He was right there!" She rushed towards the tent flap.

"Even now, you refuse to listen," Harry said, exasperated.

Jane fell silent, no longer paying attention to Harry as he continued ranting about his issues with horror stories. She moved towards the tent flap, then turned to face the door.

She knew what she had seen.

It wasn't a dream.

Harry noticed the shift in her expression and followed her gaze towards the door.

"It is locked," he said as he began unlocking it to prove his point.

As soon as the door swung open, the familiar pitch darkness stared back at them. But this time, it wasn't just the darkness. A silhouette of a man stood in the gloom, facing them. His features were hard to make out.

Harry and Jane stared at the figure, speechless, until Harry erupted, "Hey! Hey! Mister!" But the silhouette darted towards the table in the hall and leaped over it like a monkey, disappearing behind it.

Harry fumbled for the light switch and flipped it on. The hall was instantly illuminated. He rushed to the table to check for the stranger, but when he glanced behind it, there was no one there.

"What the hell?" Harry muttered, baffled. "Where did he go? He was right here."

Jane was a mess by now, her heart lodged in her throat.

"Jane, you saw him too, right?" Harry asked. Jane nodded, trembling.

Just then, his attention shifted to the entrance of the unit. A face was peeking at him from outside.

"Hey! Stop," Harry shouted, dashing after it.

Meanwhile, Jane started packing. It was too much for her to handle.

Outside, Harry turned to check every corner of the unit. There was no one there. The slow pitter-patter of rain fell on the galvanized shed nearby—the only sound breaking the silence. Just then, Jane's scream tore through the night.

Rushing back inside, Harry found Jane ready with their bags, looking as if she was about to have a nervous breakdown.

"We need to leave this place. Now," she said.

This time, Harry didn't argue.

With their bags in hand, the couple hurried towards the reception. On the way, they bumped into the attendant, who was carrying a searchlight.

"All good? Do you need something?" the attendant asked casually.

"What the hell is this place? We just saw a man who disappeared behind the desk!" Harry snapped.

The attendant didn't seem surprised.

"Oh, that! You're not the first person to say that."

Harry grabbed him by the collar. "Why didn't you tell us what was going on here?"

The attendant quickly retorted, "What? And miss out on a thousand bucks?"

Harry was more enraged by his answer. He pointed at Jane. "Look at my wife!"

Then, he shoved the attendant against the wall, "If something happens to her, I will shut this place down. Do you understand? Do you?"

The attendant nodded meekly.

"Harry, let's go!" Jane urged.

Harry released the attendant, grabbed their bags, and started towards the exit.

Suddenly, he was reminded of Jenkins and his family. Concerned, he turned back to ask the attendant which unit they were staying in.

To his surprise, the attendant started laughing.

Harry and Jane exchanged confused glances. The attendant smirked. "I knew you were crazy. There is no one named Jenkins here. You're the only family that checked in today."

Utter shock coursed through Harry.

"That's not possible… We had…we had dinner together. They were sitting with us…"

That was enough for Jane. She bolted towards the car.

"Jane! Jane! Stop!" Harry called after her.

The attendant's laughter echoed through the void they were leaving behind.

Harry ran past Jane and unlocked the car. She quickly got in. As Harry rushed to the driver's seat, the electricity cut out, plunging the entire place into darkness.

"Was it even there in the first place?" Harry muttered, glancing at the Adventure-X signboard, now barely visible.

"Hurry!" Jane shouted.

Harry jumped in and slammed his foot on the throttle. The engine roared to life. As they drove past the main gate, the car's headlights illuminated a security guard standing beside it.

"Didn't see him before," Harry whispered.

As they passed him, both Harry and Jane turned to glance at his face, only to find that he had no eyes. Blood dripped from his empty sockets as he stared in their direction, as if he could see them.

Jane buried herself in Harry's lap, sobbing, as he consoled her, "Don't worry, honey! We're getting out of here."

They had barely hit the road when Jane's unease returned at the sight of a little girl walking alone. As the headlights illuminated her, she turned to face the car, raising a bloodstained hand as if pleading for them to stop.

"Don't stop! Oh, please, don't stop!" Jane was on the verge of a breakdown.

Harry stole a furtive glance at the girl. She looked desperate, silently imploring them for help. A deep, irrepressible urge to stop gnawed at him, but Jane clutched his arm, her voice frantic.

"Keep driving! Don't even think about it!"

They sped past the girl, but guilt settled like a weight in Harry's chest. His hands tightened around the steering wheel.

"Jane, hold on. Let's think rationally," he said, slowing the car. "She was just a child. What if she really needs help?"

"After everything we saw?" Jane's voice was raw with fear. "We are NOT having this conversation. You keep driving until we get home."

Harry tried to shake off the thought, but something about the girl's sorrow lingered. In that brief moment, when their eyes met, he felt as if she had spoken to him. And somehow, he had understood.

"Jane. I'm just saying…"

"No," Jane cut him off. "Listen to me. You are NOT stopping this car anywhere. Do you understand?"

Harry opened his mouth to respond—then slammed it shut.

Because there she was. The little girl stood at the next turn, exactly where their headlights hit. Once again, she lifted her bloodstained hands, silently begging them to stop.

"Oh God, no!" Jane gasped, gripping Harry's arm.

Without hesitation, Harry floored the accelerator, keeping his gaze fixed ahead, refusing to make eye contact as they sped past her again.

They drove in silence for half an hour until the road straightened. Jane exhaled in relief. She spurted out, "Eight."

Harry frowned, "What?"

Jane's voice was quiet but certain. "Eight murders. Remember? She was the eighth one, I think."

Harry mentally retraced everything he had witnessed that night. He understood. But he didn't respond. Instead, he reached over and placed a comforting hand on Jane's shoulder. She leaned into it, exhausted, before drifting into a restless sleep.

The distant glow of city lights seared through the night, bringing Harry a sense of relief. He eased the car's speed, breathing deeply.

Then, instinctively, he adjusted the rearview mirror.

And froze.

The little girl sat in the back seat, silent.

Harry swallowed hard, darting a glance at Jane. She was fast asleep, blissfully unaware. His pulse pounded, but he forced himself to remain calm.

All through the drive, he stole glances at the rearview mirror. The girl didn't move, didn't make a sound. She simply sat there, as if hitching a ride to some unknown destination.

As if she had finally found someone willing to listen.

An hour later, Harry pulled over, exhaling shakily. But when he looked up, his breath caught in his throat.

Somehow, he had driven past the entrance of Adventure-X again.

# DOORBELL

Anshi woke up in the basement, finding herself lying on the floor. Convinced that she had been sleepwalking again, the 24-year-old clambered towards her room. She was so drowsy that she could barely keep her eyes open, just enough to see where she was heading. Upon reaching her bed, she buried herself under the covers and was snoring in no time.

When the doorbell rang for the first time, the clock read 7 AM. Anshi was a deep sleeper, but the shrill noise was enough to stir her awake. A second ring was all it took to get her on her feet. Subconsciously, she knew it was the milkman. She made her way to the kitchen, grabbed a utensil, and headed towards the door. But when she opened it, no one was there. With a blank expression, Anshi shut the door and returned to bed.

Hardly a minute later, the doorbell rang again. Vexation painted her face as she yanked the door open, only to find the corridor empty once more. This time, she peeked outside, scanning left and right. Nothing. Annoyed, Anshi trudged back to bed. Whoever was playing this prank was going to regret it if she caught them. It was far too early for this nonsense.

At 9 AM, just as she was about to wake up, there it was again—the doorbell with its intrusive noise.

Anshi was now certain someone was messing with her. This time, when she opened the door, she stepped out, determined to catch the culprit. She walked down the corridor, glancing in both directions before moving towards the stairs at the end of the building.

The old six-story apartment housed six units on each floor. Situated near a big garden, the society was nestled in a well-established region of Mumbai, Maharashtra. It was a gated society with a watchman stationed at the entrance at all times. The residents knew each other well, often coming together for events and festivals.

Anshi lived with her parents on the third floor. But now, she stood perplexed on the stairs leading to the fourth floor, scanning for the prankster. Finding no one, she turned to descend when she spotted a small girl standing by the railing, lost in thought.

*"She couldn't possibly be the one doing this,"* Anshi thought to herself.

She hesitated before asking, "Did you ring my doorbell?"

The little girl turned to look at her but remained silent, staring blankly. Unable to elicit a response, Anshi walked back to her floor, wondering if the child was even tall enough to reach the doorbell.

This time, she didn't return to bed. Instead, she grabbed a club, determined to catch the culprit red-handed. Standing right next to the door, she waited patiently.

Fifteen minutes passed. Anshi was beginning to doubt if the prankster would strike again when—Ding-dong!

Almost reflexively, she flung the door open, shouting, "Gotcha!"

To her surprise, the corridor was empty. She rushed out, scanning every corner.

*"How the hell is this even happening?"* she burst out.

Fear settled over her like a dark cloud. Her first instinct was to call her parents, who were visiting her aunt in Darjeeling. She reached for her phone—no signal. Messages failed to send. The landline was dead.

Anshi hurried to the living room, switching on the TV. Static filled the screen.

And then—Ding-dong!

The doorbell rang again louder than ever. Terror slithered through her body.

Reluctantly, she got up from her seat and approached the door, focusing on the sill, searching for shifting shadows—any sign that someone was standing on the other side. But there was nothing.

Finally, she opened the door and remained outside, impaired by fear. Her gaze shifted to the shoddy doorbell. Hesitantly, she pressed the button. The familiar loud chime reverberated through the corridor, drowning every other sound that could have been lingering in the backdrop. She pressed it multiple times to confirm.

*"Looks fine... Maybe there's some internal issue,"* she reasoned.

Determined to get to the bottom of it, she made her way downstairs to call the watchman, who often helped with household maintenance.

"Rajesh! Rajesh!" she called out, but there was no response.

Irritated, she yelled, "Watchman!"

A man sprang from his seat and hurried towards her.

Realising he wasn't Rajesh, the usual guard, Anshi frowned, "Where's Rajesh?"

The man looked at her, bewildered.

"Rajesh....who?"

"Rajesh, the watchman?" she repeated, exasperated.

"I am the watchman, madam," the perplexed man replied.

Anshi was puzzled but let the thought slide, given the urgency of her situation. She continued, "Could you please send someone to check the doorbell in my flat? There seems to be a problem. It's been driving me nuts."

"I will get it checked, madam," the watchman assured her.

She was about to turn away when she hesitated.

"Do you know anything about the TV signal?"

The new watchman looked just as confused.

"Give me your phone," she asked, hoping to call her parents.

"Sorry, madam, I don't own a phone," he replied.

Anshi glanced at his murky clothes, regretting the request.

"Alright, just send someone. Thanks," she said before heading back.

Her retreat was slow and awkward, her head flooded with unease. The thought of returning to her room alone perched on the edge of her mind. To make matters worse, the damn doorbell wouldn't stop ringing. She changed her mind and chose to go for a walk instead.

Out in the park, she strolled for a while. Overwhelmed by the day's events, she finally sat on a bench, lost in thought. She was so distracted that she failed to notice a man sitting on the other end.

"Sir? How are you?" she asked, recognising him as her college professor.

The professor didn't respond. He kept staring at the grass ahead, seemingly lost.

"Sir! It's me, Anshi," she tried again, her voice crackling slightly.

Still, he didn't budge.

"Sir, are you alright?" She hesitated, then gently touched his shoulder, remembering he had a heart condition.

The professor's reverie broke. He looked at her for the first time, tears streaming down his face.

Anshi was taken aback. She had never seen him like this—he was usually so full of energy.

He buried his face in his palms and started sobbing, louder this time. Thrown off by his sudden breakdown, Anshi stood up and looked around, wondering if anyone else was witnessing a grown man cry.

She tried to console him, "Sir…sir, it's okay. What's wrong? What happened?"

Without a word, the professor suddenly stood up and walked away.

"Sir… sir, wait!" she called after him, but he didn't seem to hear.

He was gone, leaving her with a dozen questions.

"What a day," she muttered before heading back to her apartment.

On the way, she noticed the main gate was unguarded. The watchman was nowhere to be seen. Hoping he had gone to call the electrician, she headed for the stairs.

That's when she saw her again—the same little girl from earlier, standing by the railing, tears slipping down her cheeks.

Anshi crouched down. "What happened, dear? Why are you crying?"

The little girl wiped her tears. "Have you seen my mommy?"

Her voice was innocent, and Anshi felt her heart sink.

"What's your name?" she asked gently.

"Jia," came the reply.

Where do you live, Jia?"

The little girl pointed to a house on the same floor.

Anshi took her to the door. Jia stretched up to the doorbell, showing how she was too short to reach it.

Anshi rang it for her. They waited, but no one answered.

She turned the knob. The door clicked open. It wasn't locked.

Inside, the house was eerily silent.

Jia ran straight to her room and hugged a large teddy bear. "I missed you," she squealed, squeezing it tightly.

Anshi wandered through the apartment.

*"How could someone leave a little girl alone like this?*

She urged Jia to come with her, but the child refused. She would rather wait at home than go with a stranger.

Reluctantly, Anshi returned to her own flat, uneasy about leaving Jia alone. She threw herself onto the bed, grabbing her favourite book. Maybe reading would help take her mind off the day's strange events.

She had only finished the first paragraph when—

There it was again.

The doorbell. Shrill as ever.

Thinking it might be the electrician, she rushed to open the door.

But there was nobody there.

"Bloody hell!" Anshi screamed in frustration.

She kept the door open this time, determined to catch the culprit if it had been a prank all along. Sitting across from the entrance, she turned on the TV, flipping through channels—static on every one. The flickering screen mirrored the disarray in her mind.

Minutes stretched into what felt like hours, but the doorbell didn't ring. It seemed to be testing Anshi's patience. The static on the TV appeared to mock her now. Annoyed by the constant buzz, she got up and hit the TV hard. The flower vase on top of it toppled over, but the static persisted.

Anshi shut the door again and ran towards her room angrily. The piercing noise of the doorbell kept ringing in her head. She buried her face in the pillow, pulled the blankets over herself, and started crying. She wanted to sleep—to escape the nightmare— but she couldn't. The noise was lodged inside her brain. Her head had turned into a doorbell, ringing incessantly.

*"Why is it ringing? Why is there nobody at the door?"* she whispered, worn out by the weight of her questions.

Suddenly, it felt as if someone had jumped on the bed right next to her. She turned immediately, but there was no one there.

Terrified at the thought of a ghost in her house, Anshi frantically bolted out of the room and rushed through the nearest door—the basement. She descended the stairs until she stumbled on something and fell. She turned around to see what it was.

Anshi was too shocked to scream. Hit by trauma, her eyes remained wide as she tried to get away, scampering in disbelief and shrieking at the top of her lungs.

It was about 4 AM when the Suris returned from their vacation. A tour had always been on the cards, and Darjeeling had been the perfect destination. The fact that they didn't have to stay in a hotel was an added perk.

Not wanting to disturb their daughter, who was probably still asleep, the Suris used their spare keys to enter the house. Shikha Suri, a beautiful and hardworking woman, took great pride in maintaining the home. Even in her forties, her face barely showed any wrinkles. Her husband, Mahesh Suri, a banker by profession, was in his fifties. In contrast to Shikha, his body perfectly reflected his age.

Shikha noticed that Anshi's door was closed, just the way her daughter liked it, and scoffed at the thought of an unnecessary argument early in the morning. Any such discussion could wait—she was exhausted. Having barely slept on the journey home, she immediately headed for the bedroom. Mahesh decided to let their return be a surprise and went straight to bed as well.

Around 7 AM, their doorbell rang. Shikha tried to shake Mahesh awake, but he kept snoring. Cursing as the doorbell rang a second time, she grabbed a utensil from the kitchen, knowing it was the milkman.

"How many times have I told you to ring just once? It's Anshi's sleeping time. She gets really annoyed," Shikha complained as she opened the door to a grinning milkman.

The milkman chuckled. "Sorry, madam, I forgot. Next time, I'll remember."

"You always say that," Shikha grimaced before shutting the door and returning to bed.

Soon, the doorbell rang again. Shikha pinched Mahesh, but he didn't budge, leaving her no choice but to tend to the door once more.

It was the newspaperman, asking for the month's due. Too tired to go looking for her purse, Shikha asked him to come back the next day. Before heading back to bed, she finally managed to wake Mahesh. He got up for his routine walk in the nearby park.

Shikha was already up when Mahesh returned. As she welcomed him with his morning tea and newspaper, she noticed something was off. Mahesh looked agitated.

"What's the matter, dear?" she inquired.

"I met Mikesh in the park. He told me about Mishraji's girl," Mahesh replied, his expression heavy with concern.

"What happened to her?" Shikha fretted.

"She's been missing for the past four days. Still no news," Mahesh said.

Shikha didn't know what to say.

Mahesh continued, "I will go check on him. Everyone in the building must have visited him by now."

Mahesh stepped out but returned almost immediately, ringing the doorbell. He had been sweating profusely and needed a fresh pair of clothes. Once he was ready, he left again to meet Mr. Mishra.

Shikha got busy with her household chores. She was in the bathroom when she heard the doorbell ring. Then it rang again. Then, with a bizarre sense of urgency, it wouldn't stop.

"Coming!" she shouted, rushing to open the door— but there was no one there. Too busy to care, Shikha shut the door and continued her work. As she passed Anshi's room, she knocked.

"Anshi! Get up! It's 10 AM already!"

After finishing her morning routine, Shikha was in the kitchen preparing breakfast when the doorbell rang again. This time, it was Mahesh. As soon as the door opened, he began telling her about the plight of the Mishras—how Mrs. Mishra was still suffering a complete breakdown while Mr. Mishra struggled to hold himself together.

They were in the kitchen when a sudden crashing sound startled them.

Mahesh walked into the drawing room to find their flower vase shattered on the floor. A bit confused but too preoccupied to dwell on it, he was about to resume his story when a thought struck him.

"Where's Anshi?" he asked.

"In her room! Go wake her up! It's 10 AM, and the queen is still asleep! It's all because of your pampering that she does whatever she feels like," Shikha complained.

Ignoring her usual nagging, Mahesh knocked on Anshi's door three times before opening it. He found his daughter buried under a pile of blankets and decided to wake her up by jumping on the bed.

As soon as he did, the blanket unfurled. Anshi wasn't there.

"What?" Mahesh was bewildered.

He rushed out, yelling, "Anshi! Anshi!"

Frantically, he began checking every room.

"What happened?" Shikha called from behind.

Mahesh was already trembling when he said, "Anshi is not in her room."

"What? Then where is she?" Shikha joined him in panic.

They searched every room, every bathroom—even the beds and cupboards weren't spared. A shivering Shikha walked in, clutching Anshi's mobile phone.

"She never goes anywhere without it," she whispered before breaking into sobs.

"Maybe she went out with her friends," Mahesh tried hard to stay optimistic.

"And left her phone behind?" Shikha shot back.

Mahesh had no answer.

As he racked his brain for places they hadn't checked, his eyes fell on the basement door. Without a second thought, he rushed towards it and flung it open. The moment he stepped inside, his knees buckled beneath him.

There, lying lifeless on the cold ground, was Anshi.

Anshi stared at her own body, and everything clicked. The realisation struck her like a bolt of lightning—she had been dead all along.

She collapsed, sobbing, struggling to piece together what had happened. But no matter how hard she tried, she couldn't remember. Only the events of the day played in her mind like a broken record.

*"What was that dream I had while sleeping?"* she struggled to recall.

Faint memories slipped away until her corpse drew her attention back. The sight sent a shudder through her. She slowly stood up and shuffled towards the main door.

She sat beneath the doorbell, burying her face in her hands.

A soft tug on her sleeve made her look up. Jia stood before her, clutching her teddy bear.

"I think there's a ghost in my house," Jia whispered.

Anshi gazed at the little girl with sorrow. "You don't even know, you poor soul," she murmured, pulling Jia into a tight hug.

Just then, the doorbell rang again. It tolled like a foreboding knell.

Anshi wiped her tears, stood up, and turned towards the house. Then, she pressed the doorbell.

And waited.

Waited for the door to open.

# The Floor is Rava

Edna Thorpe, a middle-aged woman, sat on a tattered chair in her one-room rental, sipping her early morning tea. Loose strands of her uncombed golden hair glistened in the sunlight that peeked through the window. Like every night before, this one had been rough.

Dark circles had formed around her eyes, a result of the meagre sleep she had been getting since her kids were taken away. A divorced mother of three beautiful children, Edna had been a policewoman married to a judge from the city court. She stood no chance against her ex-husband, Preston Thorpe, who easily gained custody of their children. There was nothing she could do. Her defence was undermined by her frequent absences from her children's lives due to her job, one of the key arguments Preston had exploited to win the court battle.

Preston's wealth had grown substantially after he began receiving alimony. It was later revealed to Edna that Preston had already been dating a woman from Canterbury during the court trials. Five months later, he moved into a large mansion in Canterbury with his new love interest and the kids. It was widely believed that one of his primary reasons for relocating was to put as much distance as possible between himself and Edna.

But Edna was convinced that, despite being well cared for, the kids couldn't possibly be happy with Preston. Last night, when she spoke to Jilian, her eldest daughter, she could hear only desolation in her voice.

*"What was it that Jilian had said?"* she tried to remember.

*"I feel as if we are constantly being pulled down,"* Jillian had described her life at Preston's house.

Some papers fluttered on the table beside her. Her transfer papers caught her eye. The name *Northumberland* was visible beneath a stamped red seal. She had barely finished her tea when a shrill noise broke her reverie. It was far too early for a phone call. A little vexed, having just gotten comfortable, she shifted towards the corner of her cramped room where the phone sat. Her hands shook as she picked it up.

Five seconds later, she was in her car, a holster hidden beneath her jacket. She left the house with urgency and sped onto the highway.

She muttered, *"My kids need me. I will always be there for them,"* as she floored the gas pedal.

The Thorpe house was a lavish mansion nestled in the countryside near Chilham, Canterbury, in the UK. An old yet magnificent edifice, it showcased exceptional masonry, seamlessly blending wood and stone. The mansion boasted six master bedrooms, leading into an opulent dining hall and an expansive drawing room, capable of hosting over a hundred guests. Exemplifying archaic British architecture, its walls were adorned with artworks depicting renowned moments in history.

The grandeur of the estate extended to a porch that rolled down into a vast garden, bordered by a gravel road leading to a towering gate. At the centre of the garden, a grand fountain enhanced the estate's splendor. The mansion's beauty was undeniable, making the long journey through the surrounding woods a minor inconvenience.

Preston Thorpe, a 55-year-old honorary judge at the city court, was one of Chilham's wealthiest residents. The divorced man lived with his three children and half a dozen servants. His ex-wife, Edna, whom he considered delirious, lived in London, approximately 60 miles away from The Thorpe mansion.

His children included Jilian, a sharp and independent 12-year-old who saw herself as a grown-up; Carmel, her affectionate 7-year-old sister; and Arthur, the cheerful 5-year-old youngest sibling. Both Carmel and Arthur looked up to Jillian for everything. The children were home-tutored by a local teacher.

That morning, a frantic call from Arthur had left Edna aghast. She could hear loud noises in the background and felt compelled to check what the commotion was about. She never trusted Preston with the kids, and a call at such an early hour had deeply startled her.

When Edna reached the Thorpe mansion, she found its massive, ornate gate wide open. She drove slowly up the driveway, assessing the situation. The windows were shut, showing no signs of intrusion. The main door appeared to be locked. The entire environment was engulfed in silence.

The driveway led her to the front porch, where she shut off the engine and stepped out. The crunch of her boots against the gravel shattered the monotony of the stillness. Beneath the ground, something heard the footfall and stormed towards her. A hissing noise followed as it pounced in her direction.

As the creature lunged, Edna, unaware, stepped onto the staircase. Instantly, the creature halted, abandoning the chase.

She turned around, puzzled by the sound. Scanning the large garden, she noticed the fountain was no longer functional. Turning back towards the porch, she observed that it hadn't been swept.

"*Where is everybody?*" she wondered as she stepped forward.

Just before placing her foot on the doormat, the same hissing noise returned. She spun around to look again—nothing.

Edna rang the doorbell. The Thorpe mansion reverberated as if waking from a slumber. The bell chimed and then fell silent. She rang it again and waited before bellowing, "Hello! Is anybody there?"

It was a large oak door, and her voice could barely have made it through. She tried pushing it open, and to her surprise, it gave way. Suddenly, screams erupted from inside.

Edna saw Carla standing on the sofa, jumping; Jillian, the eldest, was frozen on the staircase, while Arthur, the youngest, sat on a side table across the hall.

"What? What?" Edna was perplexed.

She was about to step inside when the children shouted again in unison, stopping her from something she couldn't yet fathom. Their terror was real—they weren't playing around.

"Okay, calm down, everybody. Carla, you go first!" Edna tried pulling Carla aside from the clamour so she could hear her clearly.

Carla pointed and screamed, "Mom! Don't put your foot there!"

Edna stared at the empty floor, then looked up, "Okay... where and why?"

"Rava will get you! Rava will..."

Jillian and Arthur chimed in again, their voices rising into another frantic commotion.

"I'm going to stay right here, but one at a time. Jillian?" Edna asked, motioning for the others to be quiet.

"Mom! Listen carefully! This is serious—your life depends on your next step. No matter what, do NOT step on the floor. I repeat: your feet must not touch the ground."

Edna looked down. She was standing on a large mat. She lanced around. To her, it seemed like a normal morning.

*"Isn't it too early for the kids to be this worked up?"* she thought.

Jillian must have sensed Edna's scepticism because she reiterated, "Do not, under any condition, step on the floor. We've already lost many people today. We can't lose you too." A tear rolled down her cheek.

Edna felt amused—not because of how absurd their request sounded, but because such serious words were coming from her little girl. Her heart swelled with emotion. She longed to hug her daughter.

Ignoring the warning, she took a step forward. The children's screams erupted again, this time so frantic that they began jumping in panic.

As Edna's foot descended, a wheezing sound emanated from deep beneath the floor, as if something had been waiting for this exact moment. The instant her foot touched the ground, the floor beneath it began to dematerialise, and something emerged.

It had vaguely human features—long, dark hair, large eyes, a small nose—but an impossibly wide mouth.

This thing was not of this world. It had no body, only darkness extending below its head. Its mouth gaped open, stretching far beyond normal human limits, revealing rows of jagged, monstrous teeth as it lunged at Edna's leg.

In that split second, Edna realised the children weren't making up stories.

She lost her balance and barely managed to reach for her gun before the creature's gaping mouth clamped down on her leg, severing it with a sickening crunch.

A pain unlike anything she had ever experienced tore through her.

Overwhelmed by agony and regret, Edna pulled out her gun and aimed at the creature's head—it was already creeping higher towards her knee. She could no longer feel her lower leg, only a searing, mind-numbing agony where it had been.

Bang! Bang!

The deafening shots echoed through the mansion.

Edna looked at the monster. Her bullets had passed through it, vanishing into the netherworld, yet the entity continued crawling up her leg. She glanced helplessly at the children, who had covered their ears against the gunfire.

Just as her vision blurred, on the verge of passing out, Arthur leapt onto the floor.

"Rava, here!" he yelled, before dashing towards the staircase where Jillian stood.

The monster instantly released Edna and sprang towards the fresh pair of feet that had touched the ground.

Clinging to the door for support, Edna fought to stay upright, desperate to avoid falling onto the semi-liquid floor, which was already solidifying back to normal.

Edna couldn't keep her eyes open. The sudden loss of blood was making her faint. She looked at Carla, who was beckoning her towards the sofa. A furtive glance at Arthur showed the boy being chased by the distracted monster. Jillian was screaming at the top of her lungs, furious at Arthur's recklessness.

Before she lost consciousness, Edna made a desperate run for the sofa, hopping on her good leg before collapsing onto it. The last thing she remembered was Carla pulling her injured leg up with all her might so that her entire body was safely aboard. Then, Carla began tying the sofa throw around her wounded leg.

When Edna opened her eyes, it was so peaceful outside that she wondered if it had all been a nightmare. She turned towards the windows. It was almost dark.

*"How long was I out?"* she thought.

She shifted slightly and noticed Carla sitting beside her, sobbing. The memories of the day's horrific events rushed back. Edna looked down at her right leg. A poorly draped red cloth hung from it. She was sure the sofa throw had been yellow in the morning.

She tried to lift her leg, but it wouldn't move. The memory of the monster's massive bite resurfaced, sending a wave of nausea through her. She lifted her head slightly and looked towards the staircase, where Arthur lay asleep in Jillian's lap. The boy appeared unharmed.

Edna gripped the armrest and struggled to sit up. The effort drew everyone's attention. Carla lunged forward and hugged her tightly, relieved that she was awake.

"Is everyone okay?" Edna asked, brushing Carla's hair with her hand.

Everyone nodded.

"Where's your father? Where are the servants?"

The despondency in their eyes told Edna the answer before anyone spoke. Silence lingered until she finally broke it.

"Why do you call it Rava?" she asked.

"Because that's her name," replied Carla, throwing up her hands as if it were the most obvious thing in the world.

"Rava Collins. She was the original owner of this mansion—the one who built it before Father acquired it," Jillian added from the other end of the hall.

Arthur stirred awake, rubbing his eyes. Edna looked at him, the boy who had risked everything to save her.

"Are you okay?" she asked softly.

Arthur gave her a big smile. "I am."

Edna needed to understand the full scope of their situation. "How do you know this?"

"We read all about her in the library books," Carla replied.

Edna followed her gaze and saw the blood seeping through the cloth on her leg. She lifted her knee painfully and asked Carla to close her eyes. With gritted teeth, she unwrapped the cloth.

Her foot was gone.

Heartbroken, she tightened the makeshift bandage around her knee, fearing infection. A cry of agony escaped her lips before she could stop it. She looked at the children's helpless faces and forced herself to steady her breathing.

"I will be alright," she said, mustering all the strength she had left.

Her gaze met Jilian's. "We will be alright. We have to be brave."

Carla hugged her again.

"It's okay! I'm here. We'll take care of this together," Edna reassured, not knowing how.

She needed backup. *The police station.*

"I have to call for help. Where's the phone?"

Carla pointed across the hall to the side table where Arthur had made the call.

"I see," Edna acknowledged.

A thought nagged her. "Wait, this creature…" she paused, recalling the name, "…Rava. Why didn't she attack Jillian on the staircase?"

"It's a raised surface. She can't reach you if you're on any elevated platform," Jillian explained calmly.

"But she'll come for you no matter what floor you're on—except the stairs. For some reason, those are safe."

"You mean she's on every floor?" Edna wondered.

"Yes! We have three floors, and she appeared on all of them," Jillian confirmed.

"Huh! That doesn't add up," Edna muttered, trying to piece it together.

"How did you get here?"

"We realised we had a better chance at survival if we helped each other. Someone has to be far enough away to lure her while the others move. Rava gets distracted easily," Jillian explained.

"We've been playing this game since we were kids, haven't we, Mom?" Arthur chimed in. "We've gotten good at it."

Edna looked down at her missing foot.

*"Running is out of the question for me."*

Her eyes locked onto the phone.

"I can do it," Arthur said, standing up.

"No!" Everyone shouted at once.

"But I can make it!" Arthur insisted.

Jillian slapped him on the head. Arthur raised his hand to retaliate but burst into tears instead.

"Hey! Hey! We can't get mad at each other, alright? This isn't just another day—this is serious," Edna scolded.

The siblings glared at each other, ready for another fight.

"We cannot, under any circumstances, turn against each other. Is that understood?" Edna's voice was firm.

Jillian nodded. Arthur sniffled and wiped his tears.

Edna turned her attention back to the floor. It looked normal now. She pulled out her handkerchief and threw it down.

Nothing happened.

The monster didn't come for it.

Carla, sitting at the far end of the long sofa, watched patiently, waiting to see what Edna would do next.

Edna noticed a drop of blood trickling from her leg and let it hang over the edge of the sofa to see what would happen. As the drop was about to fall, the floor began to dematerialise, as if the monster had sensed it. The blood vanished into the semi-liquid surface without the creature appearing.

"Looks like it reacts to human blood," Edna deduced.

She looked at Carla, who was still trying to make sense of everything.

The sofa surrounded a coffee table, scattered with a few books. Edna wondered if Carla could jump onto the table without falling. Before she could say anything, Carla was already perched on it, clinging like a monkey.

"Easy! Easy!" Edna cautioned, then asked her to throw the books one by one. Jillian and Arthur were on their feet, watching tensely. One book was too heavy, and Carla accidentally dropped it. Before she could feel bad, Edna reassured her, "It's fine."

After Carla returned to the sofa, Edna painfully pushed herself up. She placed one of the books in front of her, carefully rested her good leg on it, and waited. Within seconds, the floor beneath the book began to quiver. She quickly pulled her leg and noticed that the bottom half of the book had sunk into the floor.

"It seems you can only step on foreign objects for a short time," Edna observed.

She carefully placed the books, making sure not to space them too far apart, creating a path towards the side table where the phone was. She took Carla's small steps into account as she arranged them.

Then she turned to face her brave little girl.

"Carla, can you reach the phone without touching the floor?" Edna asked, her tone grave.

Carla nodded, determination shining in her cute, sparkly eyes.

Her first step, from the sofa to the nearest book, was slow and steady. She balanced herself perfectly, much to Edna's relief. Jillian and Arthur held their breath, their hearts pounding.

As the tremors began and the floor beneath the book appeared to dematerialise, Edna shouted, "Quick! Move to the next one!"

Carla pranced to the next book, then the next, without stopping. The entity followed, its form barely visible—a shifting silhouette within the floor, waiting for her to misstep. She hesitated on the last book, the side table seemed just out of reach from her vantage point. The floor trembled violently, and the book beneath her began sinking into it.

"Carla! Jump!" Everyone shouted in unison, watching as the creature circled the book like a shark closing in on its prey.

Carla leapt just as the book was about to be swallowed. In that split second of confusion, her hand knocked the phone off the table, landing with a dull plop as the floor rippled, absorbing it halfway. A distorted dial tone buzzed from the receiver, which now lay partially submerged, its edges dissolving into the shifting surface.

The beast instantly shifted its focus towards the fallen object, only to abandon the chase when it realised it wasn't prey. As the beast left, the floor gradually solidified once more, as if nothing had happened.

With no way to contact the outside world, the four of them remained trapped inside the mansion with the monster. Hours passed as they debated one bad idea after another. What they had witnessed was undeniably life-threatening, and Edna couldn't risk another reckless move—not with her children's lives at stake.

When all discussions proved futile, a disheartened Jillian stared at the open door. A single tear slid down her cheek as she whispered, "I think I finally understand what freedom means."

Edna's heart clenched at her eldest daughter's words. She wished she could change their reality, but there was little she could do.

Then, a distant rumbling broke the silence.

"Who could that be?" Everyone tensed.

"Whoever it is, they don't know about Rava!" Arthur shouted.

Edna's ears caught a familiar crackling noise—static from a police walkie-talkie.

"They're here!" Her emotions collided—hope and terror in equal measure.

The kids began screaming to warn, desperately trying to warn whoever was about to step out of the vehicle. But Edna knew their voices wouldn't be enough.

She stepped onto a book, then lunged for the table, shoving it with all the strength she could muster towards the open door. The table skidded forward with force, nearly reaching the threshold. A guttural cry tore from her lips as pain exploded through her body—she had spent every last ounce of energy.

When she came to her senses, she noticed that two cops had already stepped out of a vehicle. Amongst them were a man and a woman whom Edna recognised from one of the stations. The man, Peter, was stout and well-known across the country. He emerged, adjusting his belt and unholstering his gun. The policewoman, Magda, had already started creeping towards Edna's car with suspicion.

Just then, the sinister whistling noise returned. Almost immediately, Edna screamed to alert them, "Get in the car!"

Startled by the voice from the house, they looked up. In the blink of an eye, the monster erupted from the ground, lunging with a ravenous fury. It clamped its jaws around Peter's torso, lifting him off his feet. As he lost balance, his gun fired erratic shots into the air. The creature shook him here and there violently before pausing, then, in one swift motion, devouring him completely. Within seconds, it vanished back into the ground.

For a moment, silence reigned.

Edna's heart nearly stopped when she realised Carla was sitting beside her on the table—she had used the distraction to her advantage. Spinning around, Edna checked on her other children. Jillian was still on the staircase, but Arthur was nowhere in sight. Puzzled, she turned back to the terror unfolding outside.

She screamed at the top of her lungs, "Get in the car, Magda!"

Carla joined in, both of them pleading for the officer's safety.

Magda, frozen in shock, took a moment to process what was happening before snapping back to reality. She turned and sprinted towards her car. She had just managed to open the door when the monster returned—this time with unhinged aggression. It lunged unnaturally high, lifting her and the car into the air before swallowing her whole in a single bite. The car slammed into the ground, landing front-first, as the creature disappeared once more. The patch of earth that had turned to bog solidified instantly, leaving a quarter of the vehicle embedded in the ground.

The world around them lay undisturbed, betraying no sign of the carnage moments ago. Gasping for breath, Edna turned and found both Jillian and Arthur sitting at the edge of the table. She pulled them into a crushing embrace, holding them so tightly she could have smothered them. Deep down, she was tormented by the thought of their safety. What she had just witnessed was horrifying, but the mere thought of it happening to one of her children was unbearable.

"Mom! We're fine!" Arthur called out, drawing her attention to the bag he carried.

"How did you....What's in..." Edna could barely complete her sentence before Jillian unzipped the bag, revealing Arthur and Carla's toys.

The next hour was spent strategically tossing toys of all shapes and sizes onto the porch. Most were made of hard plastic, and as Edna carefully threw them, she wondered how on Earth her children's feet wouldn't get hurt. How was she supposed to step on them with just one good leg? Had no one considered that? But above all, her children's safety was her top priority.

"Kids..." Edna's voice broke as she tried to speak. She took a deep breath, steadying herself before addressing them with solemn resolve. "Listen to me carefully. No matter what happens, I want you to make it to the car. Do you understand?"

The kids nodded.

She continued, "For some reason, the porch stairs seem safe. Once you're there, wait for the rest of us. Jillian, do you remember your driving lessons?"

Edna was referring to the occasional training sessions she had given Jillian in case of emergencies.

Before Jillian could voice her hesitation, Edna handed her the keys. "I want you to take the wheel."

Then she turned to Arthur. "Arthur! Please be careful! No more rash decisions—always talk to your elders before doing anything."

"Okay, Mom!" Arthur responded quickly.

Next, she faced Carla. "Carla! You have to look after your little brother and always listen to Jillian." Carla nodded.

Finally, she turned back to Jillian. "You have to be strong, my child. They will always look up to you. Keep them in your sight at all times."

"Don't worry! I've got this," Jillian assured her.

Arthur hugged Edna tightly, "We'll get through this, Mom!"

Edna could hardly believe how much her children had matured. All this time, they had made the right choices, working together to keep each other alive. She couldn't always be there to protect them, but they had done exactly what she had always hoped for—looking out for one another.

Taking one final at the mansion, she muttered, "Let's get the hell out of this godforsaken place."

Arthur was the first to step out, nimbly hopping from toy to toy. Edna watched with her heart in her throat, but to her relief, he moved effortlessly, adjusting to the different shapes and sizes beneath his feet. Only a few toys fused with the floor, as he made it to the porch steps.

Then Carla emerged from the doorway, stepping first onto the raised threshold before placing a foot on a stuffed animal to move forward. She winced as she accidentally stepped on her favorite Barbie box, cringing at the thought of crushing it. In the background, a faint hissing noise lingered. A moment later, her foot landed on a jagged plastic toy.

"Ugh! This thing is stabbing my foot!" she complained.

"Sweetie, I know it's uncomfortable, but it'll be over soon, okay? We have to keep going. We can't let that monster win," Edna urged, tying hope to her strides.

Relief flooded Edna once Carla reached the stairs, where Arthur was anxiously bouncing in place. Now, it was Jillian's turn. Edna scanned the toys. There was still enough debris protruding from the floor for Jillian to step on, but she worried the most about her eldest. Jillian's feet were larger than her siblings', making her steps more precarious. She would have to tread carefully to avoid touching the floor.

Jillian hesitated before stepping out. At first, she moved cautiously, shifting her weight onto each toy, then pressed forward, stepping onto smaller playthings. But one toy—already partially merged into the floor—stood in her path. Avoiding it was impossible.

Edna's heart pounded. The kids on the stairs held their breath.

"Careful, Jillian!" they cried in unison.

Jillian took a step, but panic seized her. Her foot slipped. Time seemed to freeze as her heel brushed the floor.

Edna reacted instantly. She spun around and, balancing on her good leg, deliberately stomped down, shouting at the top of her lungs, "Run Jillian! Run!"

She barely managed a few hops before collapsing near the sofa, unable to go any further.

Jillian turned, locking eyes with her mother. But before she could even process what was happening, the monster erupted from beneath Edna with the same violent force that had swallowed Magda minutes earlier. The impact sent Edna crashing against the ceiling before she plummeted back down, dazed. As the creature coiled around her, Edna stopped struggling.

Her last breath was spent screaming, "Jillian, go! Get in the car! Take Arthur and Carla—drive, and never come back!"

With tears blurring her vision, Jillian grabbed her devastated siblings and ran for the car, dragging them along until they were all safely inside. Her hands trembled as she fumbled with the keys, her sobs making it harder to focus. But soon, the engine roared to life, drowning out Arthur's frantic protests and Carla's confused cries. Moments later, the car sped through the open gate.

Arthur, overwhelmed with grief, clawed at Jillian's arm, his voice breaking. "You left her!"

"She's gone!" Jillian shouted back as she slammed on the brakes, her voice edged with anguish.

Arthur shrank into the backseat, his small frame trembling. Carla had already burst into tears. Looking at Arthur—his face pale with fear and disbelief, Jillian softened her tone.

"I saw her, Arthur," she said, her voice unsteady. "The monster swallowed her. She's not coming back."

Arthur's breathing turned ragged, his chest rising and falling rapidly. A single big tear slid down his cheek, followed by another. Jillian clenched the wheel, struggling to keep herself together. "She told us to be brave."

Arthur sprang forward, throwing his arms around her. Carla followed, and together, they clung to each other, wrapped in their shared grief.

They held on until their sobs faded into silence. Arthur was the first to speak, his voice small, fragile. "What are we going to do? There's no one to take care of us now."

Carla was the next to whisper, "Are we going to be okay?"

Jillian glanced at the mansion in the rearview mirror. It looked eerily still, belying the tragedy that had just unfolded.

She tightened her grip on the wheel, inhaling deeply before answering, "We'll be okay."

# Thirteenth Floor

Gurugram, located in Haryana, India, had recently transformed into an IT hub. Many industries flourished in a very short period. Big names leased offices in towering buildings. These buildings housed more than 100 offices, accommodating a workforce of over 20,000.

One such cluster of buildings emerged near Sector 29. The hub provided every amenity one could dream of, with various shops thriving at the base of these structures. The IT crowd often thronged the area during snack breaks, helping many businesses flourish.

In the Sector 29 hub, six massive buildings stood, each with 25 floors. There were at least five to six companies on every floor. Simian Tech was one of them.

A renowned multinational company on the fourteenth floor, Simian Tech managed numerous overseas projects and was thriving financially. It was so successful that they even contracted a catering service to provide free breakfast and lunch for their employees.

The company's infrastructure was excellent, offering various facilities, including a gym, multiple conference rooms, a cafeteria, a town hall, and recreational table tennis. Large desks adorned the office, creating countless cubicles, each capable of seating four employees. Managers had separate cabins equipped with rolling curtains for privacy.

To prevent data leaks, the company implemented strict security measures and closely monitored all entrants. Every employee was issued an access card bearing their name and photograph. These cards allowed employees to pass through security doors and move in and out of the office.

Tarun Bhatia, a 24-year-old software engineer, had been working at Simian Tech for the past three years. He was a fair-looking man who preferred to keep his hair cropped short and sported a sharp French beard. As per company policy, he typically wore formal attire on workdays. An access card was always seen hanging loosely around his neck for easy accessibility. Since employees were required to bring their laptops to work, travelling meant carrying its weight on his shoulders.

Tarun had always felt that engineering was forced upon him due to his lack of career direction. Even after three years, his feelings hadn't changed. He often pondered how easily he could have become an illustrator—his first career choice—but with little say and power to swim against the current, he had ended up like his other friends, drifting towards a predetermined fate.

Visiting the same place daily can lead to a sense of ennui, and that's exactly what happened with Tarun.

He began viewing his workplace differently, always seeing beyond its grandeur. Eventually, he started to hate the place.

Every day, as he entered the establishment, he had to first make his way through the foyer towards a glass door that opened into the reception. Before entering the office, he had to pass through a metal detector, where a security guard would inspect his belongings. Once inside, he navigated sinuous passageways to reach his cubicle, where he would place his laptop bag on his desk before heading to the cafeteria to grab breakfast, where subpar food always awaited him.

Once he returned to his seat, he became fully engrossed in his project, losing himself in a world of code. A daily stand-up call tracked his progress, primarily focusing on what he had accomplished that day and what he planned to do next. By the evening, he was usually too exhausted to do anything but head straight to bed.

He did not have any friends, save for a few companions who often chit-chatted when there was nothing to do. Through their gossip, he occasionally learned something useful, though most of it was forgettable chatter.

One day, while he was busy working, one of his colleagues started discussing his new house, emphasising how *Vastu* had influenced his choice of floor. The conversation then shifted to how even their office location had been strategically chosen, keeping all factors of *Vastu* in mind.

"Do you know in *Vastu*, the number 13 is considered bad luck? That's why you never see that number anywhere," one of the guys remarked.

"No kidding!" Tarun replied, realising he had never noticed that before.

"Of course, because of Friday the 13th?" someone joked, and the conversation fizzled out.

The next day, Tarun woke up later than usual with a headache. Considering taking a half-day, he started concocting an excuse while getting ready. While hailing a cab, he noticed that the distance to his office was displayed as 13 km. Shrugging it off, he got in and reached the base of his building. He rushed towards the elevator, as there was no time to waste. A lady had entered just before him.

He pressed 14 for the floor where his office was, and was about to relax when the lady who had entered first asked him to press 13 as well. Tarun immediately reached for the elevator buttons but couldn't find the number. He searched carefully again, only to realise that floor 13 was missing. He turned around and said, "But there is no 13..."

He could barely finish his sentence when he realised there was no one behind him. He was all alone in the lift.

"*How is this possible?*" Tarun wondered, scanning each corner one by one. Even though the lift was moving up, his attention kept shifting to the empty space around him. There was nowhere to go if something dreadful happened. He felt trapped in that confined space.

*"What am I going to do?"* echoed softly in the recesses of his mind as he anxiously waited for the doors to open.

The ping of the elevator on each floor echoed like a death knell in his chest. He looked up at the display: 9, 10, 11, 12… the numbers kept climbing, much to his relief.

But then his heart nearly stopped when he realised the display had paused at 13. The elevator doors opened to a world of darkness. No lights flickered outside. His hands immediately went to the door-close button. He pressed it multiple times, but the doors wouldn't shut. He tapped 14 helplessly, but nothing happened. The lift had stopped on the thirteenth floor.

*"But there was no thirteenth floor in the building…"* Tarun tried to reason with himself.

His first instinct was to stay in the light—but for how long? He peeped out, looking first to the left, then to the right. Nothing but darkness. Just then, the light on the elevator ceiling flickered. Panicked, he rushed outside, too scared to even glance back, and headed straight for the stairs.

Pushing the latch of the door took some effort as it revealed a warren of stairs ahead. Fortunately, an old bulb was still working. The only way to go, of course, was up—that's where his office was. Relieved to have some light, Tarun started climbing the stairs. For the first time, he felt the weight of his laptop pressing down on him. It was killing him.

He had only reached the second landing when he heard a clicking noise coming from below. He peered over the handrail, only to spot a figure climbing upwards. It seemed to have emerged from the staircase door.

The figure sat on the ground, shuffling slowly from one step to the next. Then it looked up at him. Its big, brooding eyes seemed lost in the nuances of the IT world. Their eyes met, and suddenly, it lunged towards him, as if locking onto its prey.

If not for the absence of people, the fourteenth floor would have seemed like any other day. The ceiling lights were on. Emerging from the only staircase door on the floor, those lights felt blinding to Tarun. But the relief was momentary, for the clicking noise continued to chase him, drawing closer every second.

Tarun stumbled on the stairs but immediately sprang towards the glass doors of his office. The bright lights of the reception awaited him. As he approached the glass door, he instinctively reached for his chest— where his access card usually hung.

But it wasn't there.

His heart pounded as he realised it must have fallen somewhere. Only the lanyard that once held the card remained, dangling loosely like a noose around his neck.

With bated breath, he turned around, looking towards the staircase door. Silence loomed from the other end of the floor. Then, there it was again— the clicking noise. He saw the staircase door being pushed open.

That was it for Tarun. Panic surged through him. He started banging on the glass doors in utter dread, peering inside to catch the attention of anyone who could let him in. His eyes fell on a pair of worn-out shoes belonging to a security guard, suggesting that someone had been sitting right next to the door.

"Security! Security! Open the door!" he shouted at the top of his lungs. But there was no movement. The shoes remained exactly where they were.

Meanwhile, the shady figure had entered the floor and was headed straight for Tarun. His banging grew louder, so forceful that he feared he might shatter the glass with his own hands. Just then, a familiar beeping noise echoed—a sound so ingrained in his daily routine that it had nestled in his heart. The door lost its grip—someone had used their access card, allowing him to enter.

He swung the door open and got in. The first thing he noticed was the security guard in the chair. But to his horror, it was a skeleton draped in security clothes. Tarun checked the nameplate—it was the same vigilant guy who was always stationed next to the door, tending to people without access.

A loud bang on the door made him look up. The figure that had been chasing him looked like just another IT guy, dressed in dishevelled clothes. But his big, soul-piercing eyes told a different story. He drooled recklessly, desperate to get inside—to get to Tarun.

Suddenly, the figure Tarun had mistaken for a skeleton grabbed hold of his laptop bag. Tarun fought with all his might to free it, but his efforts were in vain. The dead security guard yanked the bag away, leaving Tarun no choice but to flee in terror. Trepidation dripping down his neck, he sprinted straight for the cafeteria.

In the back of his head, he remembered that it should have been breakfast time. But, when he entered the cafeteria, a ghostly stillness greeted him. There was no one inside.

His gaze fell on the food, and he immediately retched. A foul stench filled his nostrils. In one bowl, worms festered on the decaying remnants of a hen. In another, flies buzzed over moldy bread. And in the third, rats feasted on a rancid piece of meat.

Beside the cafe was the recreational area, where ping-pong tables were usually set up. The distinct sound of a ball hitting paddles echoed through the air. The noise made Tarun turn his head in that direction. But the most bizarre thing was—there was no one there. Only the ball moved, bouncing back and forth across the table.

Terror-stricken, Tarun bolted towards his seat, his mind spiraling with fear.

Only those who work night shifts truly understand how unsettling it is when the usual office bustle fades, leaving behind an eerie emptiness with only a few workers scattered around. Every noise across a table makes you look. The sound of your boots hitting the floor as you walk through the corridors, the squeaking of a chair, or the clacking of keyboard keys breaking the monotony of silence sends a chill down your spine.

The tension was palpable, made worse by the fact that Tarun didn't have his laptop with him.

*"What am I going to do?"* Tarun thought, feeling exposed and vulnerable without anything to occupy himself.

A nagging dread gnawed at him, worsened by the constant, routine walk of his project manager, who checked on the employees every few minutes.

Tarun sat on his chair, picked up a pen, and grabbed a notepad from his drawer. He started scribbling aimlessly, unable to focus on what he was writing because his attention was fixated on the cabin to his right—where his manager was usually stationed.

The cabin door squeaked open, and a monstrous skeleton emerged, draped in a loose, flowing black robe. Tarun ducked at once, pretending to be busy. The fear of not having a laptop to work on weighed heavily on his soul.

Footsteps echoed as if the manager were making his usual rounds. The monster moved through every passage, the sound of bones hitting the floor making Tarun shudder.

The creature glared into each cubicle, breathing heavily, grunting as if acknowledging invisible workers. Then, it approached the cubicle overlooking Tarun's desk. Tarun pretended to jot down a complex code logic that made absolutely no sense. He counted on his fingers, then ducked again to scribble a solution born entirely of his imagination.

While doing so, he stole a furtive glance at the skeleton. To his horror, the skull still had its eyes intact—but they were chameleon eyes, shifting in all directions, adding an extra layer of terror to its already nightmarish visage.

After what felt like an eternity, Tarun heard the rattling of bones moving away to the next cubicle. He sighed with relief, realising that he hadn't been caught. But just as he relaxed in his chair, it let out a loud squeak.

The rattling noise returned—this time more forcefully, as if the skeleton had caught him red-handed.

"Where's the report?" the monster growled.

Tarun froze, unable to comprehend the question. He fumbled for words as the creature's unsettling, fidgeting eyes suddenly locked onto him, focusing intently—as if ready to suck the soul out of him.

Before Tarun could react, it reiterated, "Where's the report?"

Guilt-ridden over his unfinished report, Tarun's vision blurred. And then—snap!—his eyes flew open. The familiar cacophony of the IT world had returned.

The office was crowded as usual. Keyboards clicked

all around him. Printers buzzed. Chairs squeaked. The clicking of touchpads and mice filled the space between the usual office chatter.

Tarun blinked, his breath still shaky, only to find his real manager standing in front of him, staring at him indignantly.

He was still asking, "The report? Where is it?"

# Stoneheart

Mankind has an innate inclination towards groupism. Leave ten people alone, and they will form at least two groups within a month. They will find reasons to hate others and find reasons to love only a few. Give them a planet, and they will draw demarcations. Give them a city, and they will lean towards building another.

This cliquish behaviour was very much evident when a builder constructed a city inside a city to separate a section of the crowd from the rest. Jaimint City, as it was called, was a misnomer, for it was more of a gated community built on a wide expanse of nearly 500 acres of land. The builder's business acumen had eyed the corporate world as an investment. So, he went on to build a commercial area specifically and surrounded it with residential complexes. All sorts of amenities were provided, including a gym, a school, a library, a vast playing area, and countless shopping complexes.

The Jaimint City model catered to people from every walk of life. However, its core residential area was primarily focused on those who could afford its high-class lifestyle. The cost of a single three-room house was too much for an average working person to afford. Even the rent benchmark was quite hefty compared to the regular city standards, too much for a single working professional to afford. Due to this, employees, especially bachelors, often split the rent for sustenance. A three-room establishment would generally be occupied by at least five bachelors.

One such flat in Jaimint City had one of its bedroom windows wide open. A loud cackle had erupted from within. The two-way breeze reeked of inebriation intermingled with merriment as six bachelors sat on the floor, circling three bottles of fine rum, six glasses and a few plates of appetizers. Their sixth roommate, who had recently moved in, had yet to understand their weekend ritual, which included drinking to escape their weekly office fatigue.

The new roommate was named Avyam, a 23-year-old bachelor from Chandigarh. He had moved to Pune to work for a multinational company located in Jaimint City. Renting a shared house was his only option due to his limited budget, especially since he wanted to live as close to his office as possible. Shifting to a house in Jaimint City also meant getting acquainted with a bunch of strangers.

It had only been a couple of days since Avyam moved in. The rest of the guys wanted to socialize with the newcomer and wheedled him into drinking.

"I've had this before. I can't get drunk," Avyam reiterated, examining the brand of the bottle.

"It's terrible, I know. It makes you forget," said Divit, a 28-year-old banker, who also happened to be the eldest among them all.

"Au contraire, it makes me remember," replied Avyam, putting the bottle down.

"Well, I remember that one night I accidentally broke a chair after drinking this and started asking who broke it the very next day," said Yogesh, a 26-year-old practising lawyer, who was also the oldest renter of the flat, ignoring Avyam's remark. The roommates laughed, recalling events from that crazy night.

Among the others were Naitik, a 23-year-old musician who liked to hum songs when he wasn't talking; Manav, a 24-year-old salesman who preferred drinking to talking; and Viraj, a graphic designer who would guzzle down a full glass with every gulp.

"Have a peg! No one is forcing you to drink more than that," urged Naitik, offering Avyam a glass and breaking one of their routine rounds.

"No, I'm good," replied Avyam calmly.

"Oh, c'mon! Have at least one glass. Everyone's a professional here except Viraj," mocked Divit.

Viraj, who had gulped down his glass, burped before looking blankly at the others. Their tittering stopped when Viraj, in all seriousness, reasoned, "I notice you have a little cold. It's a medicine. People all over the world have it to stay warm."

"We still have two bottles to go, man! There's plenty," offered Manav, finally breaking his silence. He had had a few glasses in him to start talking.

"Okay, fine, I think there's no harm in having just one," Avyam finally gave in to their persistence. The glasses clinked as the evening geared up for the night.

Viraj had been telling everyone a story about his high school romance when the focus shifted towards Avyam.

"What about you? Anything interesting happened yet?" Naitik asked with a risqué approach.

Avyam looked up from his glass. He was reluctant at first to share, but since he wanted to make new friends in a new city, he decided to break the silence.

"If you're asking if I've been in love, then yes, I was in a very serious relationship with a girl during my college days," replied Avyam calmly.

"What happened?" Divit asked inquisitively.

"Nothing really happened. She just moved on," Avyam finished his glass. He looked at the puzzled brows before continuing, "Turned out she was already dating some guy and had forgotten to tell me."

"What?" Yogesh was confused.

"We had a call where I begged her to stay, despite what had happened, you know, despite knowing the truth. But she still broke up with me as if it was my fault," explained Avyam.

"On a call?" gasped Yogesh.

"Yup!" came the reply.

"That freaking monster!" exclaimed Manav.

"You know, it was quite a traumatic moment for me because, somewhere, I was unprepared for it. My heart refused to believe what was happening, I kept clinging to her like a child to a plaything," Avyam continued to recall.

"No!" replied Viraj in disbelief.

"But she remained adamant in her decision. That was also the first time I'd seen her that cold," Avyam revisited the jitters with a memory.

He was staring at his empty glass when Divit replied, "Probably a slave to the obsessive impatience of new love. Sorry mate!"

"Don't be, it was a long time ago," replied Avyam calmly.

"Must have been tough," said Manav.

"Yup, it was quite a disturbing experience," concurred Avyam.

"To the cruelty!" Viraj emptied his glass with a toast.

Avyam was still in his thoughts when he said, "I thought she loved me. Apparently, she did not."

There was silence in the room as everyone heard Avyam's voice break. He had brought everyone down.

"Hit him another!" exclaimed Naitik, breaking the silence.

"You seriously need a drink!" Yogesh shook his head as he poured another one for Avyam.

"No, I don't," Avyam tried, pulling his glass away.

"Bro! Just one more!" insisted Divit.

"No, man, please," replied Avyam as a few drops of rum spilled.

"It's alright, don't force him," Manav replied calmly, analyzing Avyam.

"You don't understand. You're looking at this from your perspective, but you don't know what happens after." Avyam looked serious.

"Everything is fine afterwards, all you have is a hangover, that's it!" Naitik shrugged.

"What's a hangover?" Viraj joked.

"Nothing happens in a mere two glasses, trust me!" Yogesh said as he filled Avyam's glass to the brim.

"Fine! This is the final one. I'm not going to have any more after this, otherwise…" He had barely finished his sentence when he stopped, confused after seeing something move behind the curtains.

Divit pretended to be angry, forcing the glass to his lips, "Grow up, boy! Drink!"

As he sipped, Viraj got up and started dancing, celebrating a boy becoming a man. He was putting words to a nonsensical song and singing, *"To all the suffering in the world, today we sing a song of rum and befriend our new roomie who looks glum."*

They all tried to rhyme with various contractions to cheer Avyam up. When the dust settled, Manav played a popular song from his mobile, and the rest of the gang joined in the fun. Avyam clapped for a while before being reeled into showing his moves, which were as pathetic as Viraj's.

A few minutes later, people were holding their bellies when they saw Viraj do a headstand.

"Why would he do that?" commented Manav, laughing.

"If he does that, it means no more drinks for him," Divit laughed, rolling on the floor.

"That escalated quickly!" Avyam laughed.

"He's like, 'Look, Mommy, I can do this,'" Yogesh mocked.

Everyone waited for Viraj to get down. The moment he did, pelvic thrusts followed, and the fun continued.

Half an hour later, everyone was tired, so they rounded up for another glass.

"No, I'm yet to finish," Avyam said. The exhaustion from dancing and the alcohol had already started to take effect. He got up to pee.

"Boy! Talk about a depressant," whispered Naitik when Avyam was gone.

"Let him be," Divit tried to reason.

"I know how to solve this," sneered Yogesh as he picked up what remained of their second bottle and poured it into Avyam's fairly empty glass. He then added a little water to dilute it, filling the glass to the brim.

"Don't fill it, or he'll know," whispered Viraj.

"That's genius!" commended Manav.

"I know," winked Yogesh, patting himself.

Avyam was washing his hands and looking at himself in the mirror when he thought he had heard a girl's voice. The familiarity in the tone made him a little conscious. He took a deep breath as if acknowledging a warning. He returned to his seat, having no memory of how much was left in his glass, before continuing with his drink.

The conversation shifted towards the gang's upcoming Goa plans.

"Let's go to Goa during the long weekend," stated Naitik.

"The booze is really cheap there, man!" Viraj remembered his last visit.

"For some reason, it doesn't give you a high, though," recalled Divit, who had been to Goa a couple of times.

"Probably because they dilute it," Manav reasoned.

"The whole thing is a scam, you know," Viraj added.

"I feel sleepy," remarked Avyam, his glass half-finished.

"Don't know why, but we don't feel sleepy there," Yogesh said, using Avyam's remark but ignoring his words.

"Or is it the experience that keeps you awake?" he continued, wondering.

"Go get some snacks from the kitchen," Viraj ordered Avyam, realising that his glass was ready to be refilled.

Avyam was in the kitchen when his glass was refilled without his knowledge. The glasses clinked, and random talk followed. The third bottle was almost finished. Avyam's glass was filled two more times without his knowledge when Yogesh mocked, "Hey, bro! You've only had two glasses. Please have one more."

"No, I've had enough. I'm already feeling dizzy," Avyam explained, trying his best not to lose focus.

"Bro! Come on! Onc glass!" Viraj chortled.

The rest of them were trying to hold it together.

"Yeah, bro! This is your first time with us," reasoned Naitik.

"Yeah, have one more at least," Divit coaxed.

Avyam raised his hands in refusal, "I understand everyone's reasoning and care, but you don't understand—I can't have more." His voice was firm, his expression serious.

"Things go really bad when I get drunk," he muttered, glancing at the open door. For a split second, he thought he saw someone standing there.

Manav clapped him on the back. "We've got you," he reassured Manav, motioning for Yogesh to pour another drink.

Avyam let out a quiet, reluctant sigh—his rejection barely audible—before surrendering to his final drink. Everyone struggled to raise the final toast before going for a 'bottoms up.'

The music played again. Half of them struggled to stand, swaying unsteadily. Those who attempted to dance lost their balance, their movements clumsy and wild. Boisterous laughter erupted as they stumbled and fell, the chaos fueling their amusement. Five minutes later, the room fell silent—everyone was knocked out cold.

Avyam was awakened by the soft touch of a hand on his face. When he opened his eyes, he saw all five of his roommates spread out on the floor in the same room. He got up, hoping to make it to his bedroom, which was adjacent to where they had been drinking. He managed to reach it somehow before falling prone on the king-size bed.

Avyam buried his face in the pillow while one of his hands hung casually off the bed. A pale hand of a girl clasped his hand, causing him to wake up.

Startled, he looked around the dimly lit room, wondering if it was a figment torn from a dream.

He turned around to lie on his back and gradually began drifting back to sleep.

It had only been a few minutes when he realised it was becoming difficult for him to breathe. Reluctant to wake up, he groped for a bottle of water that he thought was somewhere to his right. His hand fumbled over an ashtray, keys, and a few pens before brushing against someone's 'feet.'

His eyes snapped open as he immediately turned to his right. The feet he thought he had touched weren't there. Neither was the bottle. But when he tried to move his arm, he couldn't. It felt heavy. He gave it everything he had in him, but there was little to no movement. He thought about lifting his other arm, but that seemed stuck too. He realised he was positioned at the centre of the bed, his body sprawled out like Christ on the cross.

Suddenly, the weight on Avyam's hands increased. It felt as if he was being sucked into the bed. Something shuffled towards his left. It appeared to be atop a head, slowly approaching the edge of his bed.

Avyam's groggy eyes could only discern the dark hair that perched on top. He breathed heavily, as if sensing something impending. He searched for a familiar face in the dim light of the bulb. In that instant, the head emerged from underneath the bed, revealing a face with large, deep eyes.

"*You again!*" Avyam whispered, his body growing restless, anticipating the bad omen. The entity had the face of his ex, albeit darker. Her hair was down, partially obscuring her face and emotions.

The piercing black eyes first fixated on his left wrist. As they did, he felt his carpal bones snap. The intense agony that followed couldn't hold Avyam's attention for long, as the dark eyes had shifted towards his right hand. Though he thought he screamed, his voice was somehow muffled.

Before he could refocus on what was happening, he realised the girl had crawled onto the bed towards him. He could make out a badly stained white dress on her. With her long, sharp nails, she pierced her bosom, driving them towards her heart. There was no sign of pain as she pulled it out completely and held it in her hand.

Avyam stared at the still heart. It was made of stone. He knew what it meant and had envisioned his death. She looked at him with a death stare. Before he could react, the stone was struck against his head with unimaginable force, shattering his brain. With that, the room fell silent, as if bowing its head to a lifeless body.

The next day, Avyam woke up with a hangover. Not only did his head hurt, but his entire body ached as well. Remembering he had to go to the office that day, he began his morning routine.

www.ingramcontent.com/pod-product-compliance
Lightning Source LLC
Chambersburg PA
CBHW031019160726
47991CB00005B/1786